# A Deceitful Sun

# Adam Kivell

ISBN: 978-1-9990458-2-1
Cover Design: Adam Kivell
Edited by Brenna Bailey-Davies

# For Lisa

# CHAPTER ONE

# The Memory Remains

Daniel Harris let out a sigh of relief upon resting on a cushioned bench. He massaged his lower back and cursed the pains of middle age as a rainstorm engulfed the neighbourhood. The sun was setting, and its rays illuminated the droplets of rain in a beautiful display of amber. The scene brought with it a moment of emotional reprieve for Daniel as he caressed the edge of his mother's obituary. He wiped his tears away when he heard his eldest daughter calling his name. She found him sitting on the bench and took her usual place next to him. She nestled her head on his shoulder, gently took the obituary, and said, "Grandma was beautiful."

"Yes, she was."

"When was this picture taken?"

"Oh, I think my father took it nearly forty years ago. It was on Canada day, if I remember. We were about to head down to the beach. Me and my buddy, Josh . . ." Daniel massaged an old scar on his cheek with his thumb, trying not to outwardly show his emotion.

"I remember you telling me that Grandma gave you that scar."

"That was a long time ago, sweetheart. Shortly before Grandpa died."

"Well, they're together now, Dad. Mom sent me out here to ask you what you wanted for dinner."

"Tell her not to trouble herself. It's been a long day. Ask her to order pizza and wings from the Kilt. The rain has nearly stopped. I'll walk down and pick it up. Should be ready by the time I get there."

"Sounds like a plan."

Daniel let out a grunt as he stood up. He walked down the front steps, turned around, and said, "Sara, sweetheart."

"Yes, Dad?"

"I love you."

"I love you too."

Daniel walked toward his neighbours' worsening driveway; tree roots were parting the damaged asphalt. He snickered and remained there, transfixed, watching the rainwater collect in the gutter. "Oh, Mr.

Johnston, I bet you're turning over in your grave right about now," Daniel said as he glanced at his mother's picture once more. He placed it in his pocket and continued to walk as thoughts of his youth surfaced. He scratched an itch on the back of his head and felt the scar that had long since healed.

In the summer of 1985, Mr. Johnston lived in the second-to-last house on Maple Avenue in the small town of Port Dalhousie, Ontario. Located at the bottom of a hill, the immaculate home with its red brick exterior, cream-coloured shutters, matching blinds, and recently brushed porch was his pride and joy. His freshly sealed driveway ran the length of his property and ended at a matching garage. Inside was a freshly waxed cherry-red 1962 Ford Falcon. Now retired and recently widowed, Mr. Johnston found himself consumed by his newest passion: his lawn. It was immaculately kept with perfectly straight edges and a two-inch gap between the grass and the sidewalk. Daily, he would walk the peripheral boundary and pull out any weeds or imperfections. He took his time and scoured every square inch, pleased by what he saw. That was until he came across a five-foot section, nearest to the street, where it looked as if a tire from a bicycle had removed the lush green grass and replaced it with freshly disturbed dirt. Enraged by the lack of respect for his property, Mr. Johnston grumbled to himself and questioned which one of his neighbours' children was the culprit.

He looked up and down the street that was lined with one-hundred-year-old maple trees. Their branches and leaves had grown thick enough that the canopy covered everything and shaded those suffering from the summer humidity. Their deep roots created uneven sidewalks and cracks in the asphalt, but no one complained because, in full bloom, the massive trees were a beautiful sight to behold.

Mr. Johnston was appreciating the view and had forgotten why he was so upset, but his focus returned when he heard the recognizable flapping sound made by a baseball card every time it was disturbed by the spoke of a bicycle. Upon identifying the noise, Mr. Johnston perked up and saw a young boy, the age of seven, riding his dark-blue BMX bicycle down the incline while trying to gain as much speed as he possibly could. He was wearing a plain white T-shirt stained with dirt and black shorts with socks that were pulled up to his knees. His mud-encrusted sneakers pumped the pedals faster as his short brown hair flowed backwards in the wind.

Mr. Johnston grumbled to himself and watched as the young boy, who was approaching his lawn, veered toward an exposed root, and jumped into the air. He landed on the same spot where the grass had been disturbed and squeezed his brakes only to remove another large piece of lawn. The tire skidded across his driveway before finally coming to a stop in front of his neighbours' house. Knowing full well the irritation caused by his manoeuvre, the young boy looked toward Mr. Johnston and smiled before jumping off his bike and letting it fall onto the sidewalk. He did not slow down as he entered the neighbours' house without knocking on the door.

Mr. Johnston smirked as thoughts of his own youth circulated in his mind. The memory remained and made him forgive the young boy. As he slowly returned to the present, Mr. Johnston removed a navy-blue hat from his head; it had HMCS Skeena in gold letters embroidered on the front. Now that his white buzz-cut hair was exposed, he grabbed a handkerchief from his shirt pocket and swiped it across his forehead. He said, "That kid is going to be the death of me."

He was about to go inside to pour himself a cup of tea when he heard someone violently coughing. Mr. Johnston looked around and saw his neighbour bent over the rear bumper of his car.

"That sounds pretty bad, Keith. You should get that checked out."

"Oh, hey, Dick. Didn't see you there," Keith said in between coughs. "Yeah, I've got an appointment next week."

"Good. Too bad you couldn't go sooner."

"I know, but it's Canada Day," Keith said as he packed the trunk of his car with a cooler and several folding chairs, his cough steadily worsening with every movement. He stood up straight and was a few inches taller than the roof of his car. He ran his hand across his freshly buzzed, thick brown hair and equally dense moustache.

"Where you headed?"

"The beach at Lakeside Park."

"Beautiful day for it. You're not takin' that Thompson boy with you too?"

"Josh? Yeah, I think Daniel invited him to come along."

"You know he's a bad influence. Just look at what the little prick did to my lawn."

"Everybody needs a friend, Dick. At least it gives him a break from being at home," Keith said before forcefully closing the overflowing trunk of his car; his broad chest and muscular stature made easy work of it. He approached Mr. Johnston's porch so they would not have to talk as loud.

"I heard you had to pay them a visit a few days ago."

"Yeah, you know Mrs. Jensen? She lives across the street from the Thompsons."

"Sure."

"She called in a domestic dispute after she heard screaming coming from the house. They were still arguing when I arrived. They let me in, and Cindy was sitting on the couch. She was crying and covered in bruises. Don wasn't in much better shape."

"I heard they pay more attention to a bottle of booze than that boy of theirs," Mr. Johnston said as he rested his legs, sitting in his rocking chair.

"It's not an ideal home to be raised in."

"You're too kind, Keith. They're a bunch of no-good drunkards and a menace to this neighbourhood. If it were up to me, they'd be locked away for good."

Keith smirked and said, "Well, then it's a good thing you're not enforcing the law around here."

Their conversation was interrupted when Keith heard his name. He was being summoned for breakfast. He opened the screen door to his home, looked toward Mr. Johnston, and said, "Give the kid a break the next time you see him. He's been through a lot."

"I'll think about it. You going to the Kilt later?"

"Yeah, I plan on dropping by after the fireworks."

"All right, I'll see you then. Happy Canada Day!"

"Thanks, Dick. Happy Canada Day to you too."

Keith closed the door behind him and was nearly knocked over when Daniel and Josh came running down the stairs. They were racing toward the kitchen as the smell of scrambled eggs and bacon caused everyone to salivate. Keith was the last to enter the kitchen. Marilyn's back was turned as her attention was focused on the toaster; her long brown hair draped over her shoulder. The apron she was wearing was snug against her thin frame. He crept behind her, turned his head toward the boys sitting at the table, and placed his finger over his lips.

Daniel and Josh giggled as Keith tiptoed closer before grabbing Marilyn around her waist and effortlessly lifting her off the floor.

Everyone but Marilyn started laughing. Keith was the recipient of a slap across the shoulder and a stern look. He continued to playfully poke her while saying, "Who's wearing grumpy pants?" Keith knew this technique always elicited a smile, so it was no surprise when Marilyn eventually turned around and began playing along.

"I'm wearing grumpy pants," she said while chasing Keith around the kitchen with a spatula. Daniel and Josh joined in. The three of them eventually pinned Keith in the corner. They each took turns poking Keith in the stomach, ribs, and underneath his arms. There was a fit of laughter and it did not stop until Keith surrendered.

"Okay. That's it. I've had enough," he said in between coughs. They were progressively getting worse.

"Thank goodness you're getting that cough looked at next week. You should have gone a month ago. You're too stubborn for your own good."

"I know . . . I know. Breakfast smells great," he said, trying to change the subject.

Marilyn brought everything to the table. The butter was still melting on the toast when Josh reached for a piece but received a stern look from Marilyn. He stopped with his hand above his glass of orange juice.

"No toys at the table, Daniel."

His eyes widened and his gaze veered toward his father without moving his head.

"Don't look at me, son. I might be a cop, but your mother is the law in this house," Keith said as he winked at Marilyn. She winked back.

"Sorry, Mom," Daniel said before taking the toys off the table and tossing them in the hallway.

"Daniel! Place them. Don't throw them."

Marilyn whispered something to herself then suggested they eat before their food got too cold. Soon there was a scurry of hands reaching for crispy pieces of bacon, butter-soaked toast, and scrambled eggs infused with cheddar cheese. Keith was the only one who covered his eggs with ketchup to which he always received looks of disgust. Because of stuffed mouths, conversation became minimal and before long, Daniel and Josh were being excused from the table.

They grabbed their toys and ran up the stairs and into Daniel's room. Marilyn looked toward the ceiling and followed their loud footsteps as they ran down the hallway. "No running in the house!" she yelled.

Keith finished eating and let out a sigh of exhaustion. "That was great. Time for a nap," he said jokingly.

"Nice try, mister, but we have to get going after I clean up the kitchen. I know my parents will be down at the beach waiting for us," said Marilyn.

"Is your sister going to be there?"

"Of course, she is."

"What's that thing you always say? God, grant me the . . ."

"Grant me the serenity to accept the things I cannot change, courage to change the things I can, and wisdom to know the difference."

Keith smirked, so Marilyn took the towel from the oven, wound it up, and playfully whipped him in the thigh. A pursuit ensued and they ended up on the living room couch. They started to kiss, thinking they were alone, but were quickly reminded they had a lack of privacy when they heard Daniel and Josh let out a synchronized, "Ewwwww." Keith jumped to his feet and snarled as if he was a monster and chased the boys up the stairs.

He began coughing and had to stop his pursuit. As he hacked, he placed his hand over his mouth. When he removed his hand, it contained a small amount of blood. Not wanting to be the cause for concern, Keith made his way to the bathroom and washed his hands before looking into the mirror. He regained his composure before joining Marilyn in the kitchen. She looked concerned and Keith knew why. He offered reassurance that he was well enough and a promise to not miss his appointment with the doctor, and Marilyn finished cleaning the kitchen. Once done, her voice bellowed from the bottom of the stairs, beckoning Daniel, and Josh to join them outside.

Mr. Johnston was on his porch. He waved to everyone as they got into their car and wished them an enjoyable day. Josh, seated nearest to Mr. Johnston, looked out his window and shivered at the intimidating look on Mr. Johnston's face.

Mr. Johnston quickly altered his countenance and smiled. He thought about what Keith had told him earlier and decided to accept his advice and give Josh the benefit of the doubt. However, as they began driving down the street, Josh turned around, manoeuvred his fist out the window, and stuck up his middle finger.

"That no-good kid," Mr. Johnston said as he smiled and shook his head.

"What did you do that for?" Daniel asked as he pulled Josh's hand back inside the car.

"Because he's a grumpy old codger, that's why."

"You boys cut that out back there or I'm turnin' this car around," Keith demanded as he winked at Marilyn. A moment later, he turned the radio on and the four of them started singing to "Summer of '69" by Bryan Adams.

# CHAPTER TWO

# Lakeside Park

When the Harris family plus a troublesome Josh Thompson arrived at Lakeside Park, it was already buzzing with activity. To get to the parking lot they had to drive down Main Street, but pedestrians were everywhere and a long lineup of cars heading to the same destination slowed their progress.

It was a beautiful day and the patios lining the street were filled with patrons enjoying local cuisine and cold drinks. Canada flags crisscrossed awnings as red-and-white umbrellas provided shade to those who sought it. There was a long line of children begging their parents at the ice cream shop on the corner. Next to that was a dazzling array of motorcycles parked in front of the Lion's Head pub.

Next it was a sharp left turn. The marina on the right was filled with every type of watercraft from ten-dollar dinghies to million-dollar yachts stretching down the half-mile pier until they looked like one long boat. On the left was a collection of shops, and on the corner was the old Mansion House bar and restaurant.

Keith shrugged upon noticing a seemingly full parking lot. Hoping that luck was on his side, he continued to drive up and down each row, thinking that it was a matter of time before a vacant spot was found. He gave up and was about to find a spot in town when Marilyn noticed someone leaving halfway up Hogan's Alley. Resolute, and putting his driving skills as a police officer to use, Keith managed to nestle his car into the spot and let out a conniving laugh once he shifted the car into park.

"All right. Who's ready to party?" Keith asked energetically.

There was a collective, "Me!" from Daniel and Josh in the back seat.

"I'm going to find a spot on the beach under the sun," added Marilyn as she placed her sunglasses and brimmed hat on her head.

Everyone got out of the car and Keith started unpacking the trunk. "I guess I'll bring this stuff over with you then head over to the carnival with the boys."

"Sounds good, babe," Marilyn said, already several paces away from the car.

"Daniel! Josh!" Keith yelled as he looked around but could not see where the boys had gone. He called their names once more and held up two ten-dollar bills. Seconds later, they were at his heels.

"All right, boys, these are for you. That's all you get, so make it last until the fireworks," Keith said as he raised an eyebrow and shrugged.

"Awesome! Thanks, Dad."

"Thank you, Mr. Harris."

Keith watched as Daniel and Josh ran toward the Midway. He lost sight of them after they exchanged their money for tickets. Assuming they would be able to entertain themselves for several hours, Keith locked the car and carried two armfuls of folding chairs, a large red umbrella, and a cooler. Many years before, he could easily carry such objects because of his young, sturdy body. This time, however, Keith struggled. He required several breaks between the parking lot and the beach. His laboured breathing caught the attention of several people but their attempts to assist were met with a gracious yet stubborn resistance. He stopped underneath a tree, dropped his load, and started coughing. Keith bent over and spat blood-infused saliva into the nearest bush. It was several minutes before he was able to catch his breath. When he did, he resumed his march until he was next to Marilyn.

He acknowledged her sister, Roxanne, and her parents, Mr., and Mrs. Dempsey, before setting up the large red umbrella and four folding chairs. He rested in the shade as they soaked up the sun.

"What the heck too you so long?" Roxanne grumbled as she adjusted herself. Her bleach-blonde hair looked frail and her overly tanned skin made her look twenty years older than she was. She administered another layer of sunscreen on her nose and lips.

"Not having a good day, I guess," Keith said while trying to catch his breath, but his cough worsened.

"I told him a month ago to have that looked at," Marilyn said as she opened the cooler. "Now, where's my margarita?"

"Why don't you listen to Marilyn?" Mrs. Dempsey asked. "You're so stubborn."

"It's the Polack in him," Mr. Dempsey added. "Not nearly as stubborn as a Cossak or a Jew, thank god."

9

"An Israeli Jew or one of them Zionist Jews?" Roxanne said.

"Both! Now shut up and let me enjoy the sun while it's hot."

"Don't tell your daughter to shut up," said Mrs. Dempsey as she removed her hat from her short brown curly hair that stayed in place because she used too much hair spray.

"Why not?"

"Cause she's your daughter."

"It's because she's my daughter that I can tell her to shut up. You're starting to sound like my mother, rest her soul."

"At least she had good Catholic morals. She would have never told any of her children to shut up."

"She told me to shut up all the time."

"Didn't work, did it?" Marilyn said as she received a high-five from Roxanne.

"Ah . . . both of you, quit it. Anyways, you don't have to be religious to have good morals."

"That's right," Keith said.

"Let's give a slow clap for Mr. Do-the-right-thing," Roxanne said in a low voice.

"Anyone can be a good person if they chose to be, Roxy."

"Well, I know who can't."

"Who?" Mr. Dempsey asked.

"Indians," Roxanne said.

Keith clenched his jaw and flared his nostrils but kept his opinions to himself because he knew he could not change their opinions.

"Please, don't get me started on those mooches. All they do is take our money and waste it away on booze and drugs," Mr. Dempsey said.

"And don't forget that the more children they have, the more they get from the government," said Mrs. Dempsey.

"A waste of a life, if you ask me," Roxanne said.

"No religion can save them," Marilyn added.

"They should all just be put out of their misery. Or how about this? We build walls around their land and lock the gate. And if they want to enter our land, we charge them."

"It's a good thing you're not a politician, Roxy," Keith said.

He shook his head in disgust and decided to go for a swim. "Bunch of racist pricks when they're together," he said as he waded into the water. It was colder than expected for the time of year, but that did not stop him from submersing himself. He took a deep breath and put his head underneath the water but had to quickly return to the surface because he started coughing. He covered his mouth with his hands. Keith could barely contain his cough when he noticed a larger amount of blood covering his fingers. Worried, he quickly looked around to see if anyone was near before washing off the blood in the water. He watched as it dissolved around him.

Exhausted, he reluctantly returned to his spot underneath the umbrella and was relieved upon noticing that the previous conversation had ceased. Keith remained seated until his skin was dry. He opened the cooler and took out an ice-cold can of root beer. He took a refreshing sip, tilted his head toward the Midway, and hoped that Daniel and Josh were having a better day than he was.

As Keith was thinking of ways to distance himself from his wife's family, Josh and Daniel were entertaining themselves by playing whack-a-mole, riding the tilt-a-whirl, and licking cotton candy off their fingers. They were hastily eating a hot dog before going on their favourite ride called the UFO. It was an enclosed disk that was pitch black except for a few flashing lights in the centre. The interior was filled with long red cushioned planks that had wheels attached to metal poles. As the UFO spun around, the planks would extend to the top and the g-force would press the riders against them.

Josh and Daniel anxiously waited in line. Moments later, the carny removed a blue rope that hung across the entry and indifferently ushered everyone in. Daniel and Josh found their places. It was not long before they felt the spinning motion of the UFO. They laughed and screamed as their bodies were pressed against the planks, their faces agape as their cheeks flapped. A minute later they were being ushered out, and the enthusiasm they had entering turned to regret as burps containing pieces of half-chewed hot dog were forced back down.

"What a blast!" Daniel said.

"Holy cow, that was friggin' awesome!" Josh replied.

They made their way down the platform and stood next to the King of the Hammer game, the sounds of the Midway surrounding them.

"What do you wanna do now?"

Josh reached into his pocket and said, "I'm outta tickets."

"Me too."

"Ah crap. What the heck are we supposed to do?"

"I don't know. We've still got two hours until the fireworks. We can go find my dad."

"Are you an idiot? He told us to make the ten bucks last. If we went to the beach with your family, they'd make us stay with them."

"Well, what should we do?" Daniel asked.

Josh looked around. He smiled and said, "Follow me."

Daniel, without hesitating, followed Josh until he stopped next to the game where you popped balloons by throwing darts at them.

"Look!" Josh exclaimed as he pointed to an open container filled with cash. "Just reach in a grab some money when that dumb carny has his back turned."

"Uh . . . I don't know," Daniel said as he took a step back.

"You wuss. It's easy. I'll go ask him a question and stand on the other side. When he's not looking, just reach in and take it."

"Ah . . ."

"Would you rather sit with your parents and do nothing, or go on more rides?"

"Uh . . . rides."

"You're damn right. Now, wait for my signal and just reach in. Don't think about it. Just do it."

Before Daniel could say anything, Josh was already walking to the far side of the counter. He beckoned the carny over with a question. With his back turned, Josh motioned to Daniel to move, but Daniel hesitated. Josh glared at him, so he reached over the table and grabbed a few loose bills from the top. Anxiously, he quickly pulled his arm back, but his fist clipped the top of the metal container and it crashed to the ground. The carny, with his ominous blue eyes and greasy face, looked toward Daniel. "What the hell do you think you're doing?" he said, spit flying from his mouth that was half filled with teeth. Daniel froze.

"Run!" Josh yelled as he grabbed Daniel by the arm.

They raced in between tents and around loose wires as the sound of the carny screaming dissolved into the surrounding noises of bells, whistles, and music. They hid behind a tent, thinking they had got away. Josh and Daniel started laughing as they caught their breath. Josh counted the money.

"Holy crap, Danny boy. I should call you Dan the Man. There's forty bucks here."

"What do you want to do now?" Daniel said, the burden of regret in his voice.

"Whatever we want! Follow me."

Josh led the way to the nearest vendor and purchased an exorbitant amount of caramel popcorn, salted pretzels, and pop. They found a bench next to the pier and consumed every crumb. With distended stomachs, they waited in line for more tickets and playfully burped as loud as they could. They bought twenty dollars' worth of tickets and spent the next hour in a never-ending combination of rides and games.

"It's starting to get dark, Josh. We should meet up with my parents before the fireworks start," Daniel said.

"No way, Dan the Man. We've still got ten bucks left."

"But I'm tired and my stomach doesn't feel good."

"All right, you wuss. What about we go on the carousel? It's only five cents a ride. Here, take this," said Josh as he placed a five-dollar bill in Daniel's hand.

Unable to say no, Daniel followed Josh to the old carousel. They walked around to the entrance but noticed a long line of enthusiastic, impatient youngsters—their faces pressed against the fence, hoping to see their favourite animals going around in circles.

"Oh, man. This line is way too long. It's gonna take an hour just to get on," said Josh as he looked around before smiling at Daniel. "Back there, look! We can hop the fence when it stops."

"I don't know, Josh. What about the kids waiting in line?"

"Kids, schmids, you wuss. Ready?" Josh grabbed the waist-high fence and easily leaped over it. "Come on, your turn."

Daniel grabbed the top of the fence, but his conscience told him that it was not the right thing to do. He let go of the fence and started walking away, the sound of Josh's pleas buried under the music of the carousel. He walked along the long line of children until he ended up next to the carny in charge of the gate. Daniel extended his hand and gave him the five-dollar bill.

"What's this for?" the carny asked.

"For the kids," Daniel said as he walked away; his conscience felt lighter. He continued toward the beach and started looking around for his parents when Josh snuck up and punched him in the shoulder.

"What the heck! That hurt!"

"Don't leave me hangin' like that."

"Stop breaking the rules."

"Rules are meant to be broken."

Daniel scoffed as they continued to walk down the beach. Josh harassed him about why he left until recognizing the large red umbrella with Keith standing next to it.

"There you guys are. I hope you had fun. You hungry?" Keith asked.

"Nope," they said in unison.

"Thirsty?"

"Nope, we're good, Mr. Harris. We spent a portion of the money you gave us on a hotdog and pop," Josh said, his manners returning.

"Okay then," Keith said, accepting Josh's word as the truth. If it were not for the increasing darkness, he would have noticed a look of embarrassment on Daniel's face.

Soon enough, all was forgotten as Daniel's grandparents gave him a barrage of hugs and kisses, the smell of alcohol emanating from their mouths. Roxanne took him by his waist and began tickling his sides until he threatened to pee. Thinking he would receive the same attention from his mom, Daniel sat next to her but bumped into her arm, which was balancing a full glass of ice-cold margarita.

Marilyn was known to have a short wick, and the length of said wick depended on the amount of alcohol in her system. "Jesus Christ, Daniel. Watch what you're doing. You nearly spilled my drink," she said, licking the exterior of the cup. "Go sit next to your dad, would ya?"

Keith motioned for Daniel to join him, and Josh. Daniel sat down, and his dad whispered into his ear, "Nothing personal. You know how your mom gets sometimes when she drinks."

"I know."

Daniel grabbed handfuls of sand and watched as each grain found a way out through his fingers. His mother's callous reaction was on his mind and the thought of stealing money weighed heavily on his conscience. His smile that had lasted most of the day turned into a frown and he was about to confess when he heard a loud bang.

He looked up and saw the first firework blast into the sky. What followed was a brilliant barrage of colour and noise. Each magnificent explosion was mirrored by the calm water of Lake Ontario; a golden hue encircled it from the cities and towns on its edges. Daniel was lost in the moment and had forgotten about the burden of guilt. His eyes traversed the sky in awe. During the crescendo, he felt his father grab his shoulder. He looked up and smiled.

"I love you," Keith said.

"I love you too, Dad."

There was rapturous applause from thousands of admirers, and it lasted for several minutes before the revellers began packing up their belongings. Everyone wished each other a good night and good health until the next time they saw each other.

Marilyn had difficulty walking in a straight line and all she could carry was the empty glass in her hand. Keith, lacking in energy from a draining day, was happy to be carrying an empty cooler back to the car. But just as earlier in the day, his efforts were interrupted by bouts of coughing. They made it back to their car when they heard someone yelling from the other side of the parking lot. "Stop! There they are! That's them boys that stole the money!"

Marilyn was already nodding off in the front seat and could barely comprehend what was going on. Daniel and Josh froze in terror as Keith, surprised by the accusation, tried to calm the situation by speaking with the enraged carny. A heated conversation ensued, and after several minutes of reasoning, Keith reached into his pocket and pulled out his wallet. He emptied its contents, placing whatever money he had into the hand of the furious carny. Satisfied, the carny walked away just as Daniel and Josh were on the receiving end of a nasty stare.

With heads down, they got into the back seat of the car and did not dare look up the entire ride home. When they arrived, Daniel and Josh were instructed to wait in the kitchen as Keith updated Marilyn on the unfortunate events. She rubbed her sun-burned face and said, "Can it wait until morning?"

Daniel was sent to his room after Keith advised Josh that he would be contacting his parents. Josh understood and was soon ushered out the door. He picked up his bicycle off the front yard and began pedalling up the hill. The sound of the card flapping against his spokes echoed into the distance. Keith unloaded the car and sat on his porch for several minutes. He heard the rumbling of an engine and watched as Mr. Johnston drove down his driveway in his cherry-red Ford Falcon. He rolled down his window.

"You still coming to the Kilt?" he asked.

"Yeah, I'll be down in a bit."

"Nonsense, hop in. I'll give you a ride."

Reluctantly, Keith gave in to Mr. Johnston's invitation but promised himself to speak to Daniel in the morning. He popped his head in the house and said, "Heading to the Kilt. Don't wait up for me."

"Okay," Marilyn moaned from the living room couch.

From his bedroom window, Daniel watched as his father got into Mr. Johnston's car. Believing he had dodged a bullet, he got himself ready for bed and turned on his brand-new Atari 7800 and started playing Ms. Pac-Man. Several minutes into the first level, he heard his mother coming up the stairs.

"Turn that off!" she yelled, banging on the door. "You shouldn't even be playing that after what you did."

Daniel turned down the volume until he heard a door close. He turned up the volume again. Moments later, his door was flung open; Marilyn stood in the doorway.

"I told you to turn that thing off!" she said, unplugging the cord to the television. She grabbed Daniel by the arm, dragged him into the bathroom, and stood him in front of the mirror.

"Look at yourself, Daniel! What do you see?" Marilyn said, slurring her words.

Daniel did not respond.

"You know what I see? I see a thief. I see a punk. I see a worthless kid who thinks he can do anything he wants. If you think you can get away with stealing, you're wrong. Now, go straight to bed and don't you dare think about playing that stupid game."

Daniel ran into his room, closed the door, and cried into his pillow until he fell asleep.

Down the street, Keith and Mr. Johnston arrived at their favourite pub: The Kilt and Clover. The patio was packed with people all enjoying the celebrations with food and drink. Keith opened the door and out came a massive billow of smoke. He started coughing and it caught the attention of many patrons next to the bar. A group of men looked toward him and as they recognized who it was, they shouted, "Shorty's here!" They approached him with inebriated hugs, handshakes, and a pinch to the cheek.

"Make sure the root beer is ice cold!" someone yelled from the crowd. Laughter broke out from the bar.

What followed was two hours of worth of unabridged, unhinged joke making, name calling, jeering, and drunk opinions about current affairs. Last call was announced, and Keith always took responsibility for making sure all his friends made it home safely. They packed into Mr. Johnston's car and thanked Keith as he drove each one of them home.

After returning to his own home, Keith resumed his position on the front porch. His time of contemplation was interrupted by bouts of coughing. He did not want to wake up Marilyn or Daniel, so he stepped onto his front yard where, due to pain in his chest, he ended up on his hands and knees. Keith coughed violently and spat up a large amount of blood. He gathered enough strength and, once the coughing stopped, went inside. He wiped blood and sweat from his face and looked at his reflection in the kitchen window. His bloodshot eyes were surrounded by dark rings. Wrinkles on his face became more noticeable as he tried to catch his breath.

Keith stood up straight and, for the first time since his ailment started, he became worried that something was wrong.

# CHAPTER THREE

## Toothless Will

It was unusually hot on the first day back to school. Opened windows and whirling fans did not have much effect on the temperature. So, as the bell rang signalling the end of the day, both students and teachers alike looked forward to a reprieve from the hot, stuffy classrooms.

After saying goodbye to his classmates, Daniel unlocked his bike and was about to head home when he saw a girl sitting on the swing. She was alone; her elbows were clinging to the chains and her head was resting in the palms of her hands. Daniel nervously approached and noticed she was crying.

"Is everything okay?" he asked, putting down his bike.

"No," she responded. Her long chestnut-brown hair covered her face.

"You're the new girl . . . Olivia, right? We're in the same class but I sit on the far side of the room, closest to the windows. You just moved here, didn't you?"

"Yes," she said, wiping tears from her face.

"What's wrong?"

"Oh . . . just missing my friends."

"Where did you move from?" Daniel asked as he sat on the swing next to her.

"We moved from Toronto."

"Wow! I love Toronto. It's so big. We were just in Toronto a week ago for C.N.E. They have the best waffle ice cream sandwiches. We go every year to watch the airshow."

Daniel continued to reminisce about his experiences. He neglected to notice that his own excitement was making Olivia's reality that much more painful. She continued to cry.

"Oh. I'm sorry. I guess I should keep my mouth shut," Daniel said.

"No, it's all right. My parents tell me that it takes six weeks to get used to anything new. This is week four since the move. It's just . . . it's hard for me to make friends."

"Well, we could be friends," said Daniel, wanting to cheer her up.

It worked. Olivia tucked the long strands of hair covering her face behind her ears. She looked at Daniel with teary eyes. Daniel noticed the dozen freckles adorning her cheeks. Her amber eyes were staring directly into his as she smiled, her symmetrical dimples now visible. Daniel remained motionless as a new sensation tickled his senses. He felt butterflies in his stomach when Olivia said, "I think that's a great idea. Would you like to come over to my house and play?"

"Sh-sh-sure," Daniel said nervously.

Olivia bounded out of the swing. Daniel grabbed his bike and together they began walking across the field. They talked the entire way to her house. When they arrived, Olivia's father pulled into the driveway and promptly got out of the car. He was wearing a dark-brown suit. His tie was loosened, and the upper portion of his shirt was unbuttoned. He had black hair that was parted on the left. He adjusted his glasses before picking up Olivia and swinging her around in a circle.

"You're getting so big, sweetheart. I've got to put you down," he said, placing his hand over his lower back. "And just who is this young man?"

Daniel, intimidated by his forwardness, said, "Hi, I'm Daniel Harris. It's a pleasure to meet you, Mr. Rouble."

"Well, such a polite young man you are! But please, call me William. Harris, eh? I think I've heard that name before," he said, rubbing his eyebrow. "Is your father Keith Harris? Police officer, right?"

"Yes, that's my dad."

"Oh, well then, if you're his son you are more than welcome to hang around my daughter."

"Thanks, Daddy," Olivia said, smiling. The purity of her smile could brighten anyone's day.

"You're welcome, sweetheart. Now, where's your mother? I think I smell dinner cookin'!"

"Can Daniel stay for dinner too?" Olivia asked with wide eyes.

"Well, sure he can. As long as it's okay with Daniel."

"Okay with me," Daniel said nervously.

"Great. Better call your parents to let them know where you are. There's a phone in the kitchen. Now, I've gotta get out of these work clothes. See you kids for dinner," William said as he entered the house, his whistling fading as the door closed behind him.

Daniel and Olivia continued to play outside until her mother, Natalie, a mirror image of her daughter, beckoned them to the dinner table. They hurried down the hallway, pretending to hold the other back if they were leading. Their laughter was a welcome change within the house because, since the move, Olivia's crying had been commonplace. William and Natalie looked at each other and smiled as Daniel and Olivia found their seats.

Daniel was so excited about the invitation that he forgot to call home. He enjoyed a dinner of roast beef, mashed potatoes, and carrots.

"This meat is so tender," Daniel said as he shoved a forkful of food into his mouth. "And the potatoes are so creamy. This is the best meal I've had in weeks," he continued, barely allowing himself to breathe in between bites.

Olivia giggled and said, "You sound like a dog when you're eating."

There was a moment of uncomfortable silence. Natalie looked at Olivia with a raised eyebrow. She was about to make Olivia apologize when William started snorting like a dog and said, "I love dogs! Man's best friend." Moments later he was enticing everyone to join in and it was not long until they were all laughing and snorting like dogs together.

Once everyone had full bellies and empty plates, Natalie suggested they take a break before enjoying some ice cream. Daniel was introduced to their tradition of playing a game of cards after dinner.

"Have you ever played Crazy Eights?" Olivia asked.

"A few times," Daniel said as he arranged the cards in his hand.

"Don't worry. We'll take it easy on you," William said.

Daniel was absorbed by the atmosphere. Laughter rang out as everyone took turns getting revenge on those who made the other pick-up extra cards. Daniel was entranced by William's ability to shuffle when Natalie asked, "You mentioned that it was the best meal you've had in weeks, Daniel. Is everything okay at home?" William peered over his glasses at her.

Daniel hesitated and stared at the table. He took a deep breath and said, "My dad is sick. We found out two weeks ago that he has cancer in his lungs."

Daniel's lip wobbled, and he angrily swiped at the tears escaping his eyes. Olivia was the first to give him a hug and she did not let go. Natalie and William also embraced him, and they shared in Daniel's grief. They passed around a box of tissues. Once they obtained their composure, Daniel continued, "My mom is angry all the time and she drinks a lot. I can't do anything right, and she just yells at me. So, I spend most of my time in my room."

"I'm sorry to hear that," Natalie said as she rubbed Daniel's shoulder. "People cope differently with stress, and I'm sorry to hear what's happening to your mother. I'm sure she's been going through a lot of emotions the last two weeks."

"I'm sorry too," Olivia added, wiping a tear with her finger.

"Well, if you ever need anything, Daniel, you're always welcome here. And I'd be willing to help your parents around the house," William said.

Daniel looked at each of them and smiled.

"Who's ready for ice cream?" Natalie asked.

Daniel and Olivia smiled and said, "Me!"

Spoons clanked against bowls as they enjoyed their ice cream. Daniel, basking in a reprieve from his worries, slumped in his chair after relishing the last spoonful of ice cream. He was full and let out a yawn that quickly enveloped everyone. Soon after, there was a unanimous laugh followed by William stating, "I think we should call it a night. Thank you for joining us, Daniel, but I think it's time for you to go home." They shared a group hug and William said, "Can you see Daniel to the door, sweetheart?"

"Okay, Daddy," Olivia said with a cheerful tone. She pushed Daniel's chair into the table after he stepped aside.

"Thank you for dinner, Mrs. Rouble," Daniel said.

"You're welcome, sweetie. Have a good night."

"You too."

Olivia rolled her eyes, grabbed Daniel by the waist, and pushed him down the hallway. It tickled him and he started to laugh. This continued until they were standing on the porch.

"You have really nice parents, Olivia," Daniel said. He began walking toward his bike.

"Yeah, they're all right. I bet you have nice parents, too."

"Yeah, they're all right," Daniel said, imitating Olivia.

They laughed, and before Daniel knew what was happening, Olivia kissed him on the cheek. He jolted his head back and nervously stared into Olivia's eyes. Not knowing what to do, he hopped on to his bike and started pedalling. He turned around once more to see Olivia waving. "See you tomorrow!" she yelled.

Daniel was too far to say anything, so he offered an energetic wave before rounding the corner. The sun was beginning to set by the time he got home. He placed his bike in the garage and closed the door then skipped his way to the front of the house with a smile on his face. It did not last long when he noticed his mother waiting for him. Marilyn had closed fists placed on her waist. She scrunched her eyebrows together and looked down toward Daniel.

"Where the hell have you been?" Marilyn yelled, her voice echoing down the street.

Shocked, Daniel said, "I'm sorry—"

"You're damn right, you're sorry. I drove all over the neighbourhood looking for you. Where were you? Were you at the Thompsons'? You're not allowed to play with Josh. Especially after the crap you guys pulled on Canada Day. He's a bad influence!"

"No, Mom," Daniel said. He winced, as if expecting to be struck.

"Well, where were you then?"

"The Roubles—"

"The Roubles? Who the heck are the Roubles? And what were you doing at the Roubles'?"

"Having dinner—"

"Dinner! You mean you've already eaten, too! For the sake of . . . what did I do to deserve this?" Marilyn asked, raising her hands to the sky. By this time, several neighbours began congregating on their porches. "You better not being lying to me, Daniel. Were you at the Thompsons'?"

"No, I was with Olivia. She's new at school and she invited me over to play."

"I don't believe you."

"Really! Her parents invited me to stay for dinner."

"Enough of the lies, Daniel!" Marilyn exclaimed. She took Daniel by the wrist and pulled him into the house. She continued pulling on his arm until he was looking at his reflection in the bathroom mirror.

"Now, tell me what you see," Marilyn demanded.

Daniel started crying and said, "I don't know, Mom."

"Well, I'll tell you what I see. I see a liar. I see an ungrateful kid who lies to his mother."

Marilyn was prepared to continue the barrage of insults, but she heard footsteps at the top of the stairs. She went silent and looked at Daniel, placing her finger over her lips.

"Is everything all right in there?" Keith whispered; his voice strained.

Marilyn went to the bottom of the stairs and left the bathroom door open. Daniel could hear her talking in a soft, reassuring manner. "Everything's all right, Keith. I was just worried about Daniel, but he's home now. You go back to bed and rest."

Daniel remained in the bathroom as he heard the bedroom door to his parents' room close. His heart started racing as his mother's footsteps on the stairs got louder. Soon, she was blocking the doorway. She clenched her jaw and spoke through her teeth. "Don't you ever lie to me again. Now, go upstairs and say good night to your father. You go straight to your bedroom when you're done, understand?"

"Yes, Mom," Daniel said as he looked to the floor. He did not dare make eye contact. As he slowly climbed the stairs, he could hear the clanking of ice being placed into a glass followed by the sound of a bottle being unscrewed and its contents being poured. Daniel sighed and continued up the stairs.

He gently knocked on his father's bedroom door before going inside. The room was dark except for a light on in the closet. Daniel scoured the room. Keith was lying on his side of the bed, and Daniel watched him as he slept. He rested against the door frame and began to think about how much had changed. Once chemotherapy had begun, his once energetic, funny, and supportive father slowly become lethargic and destitute. Happy memories were being overcome by current realities and no one within the Harris household had any reason to cling to hope or have faith that life would improve.

This new normal continued for the following month and the only thing Daniel was looking forward to was Halloween. Although, he did find an escape whenever he was invited to the Roubles'. He and Olivia would spend time together after school. Sometimes she would ride on the back of Daniel's bike. Other times, they could be seen holding hands as they walked in stride.

Marilyn continued to doubt Daniel's whereabouts. She was regularly seen waiting for him on the porch, the condensation from her glass collecting on the banister. One night, she was ready to unleash a torrent of anger, but her countenance changed when she watched a car stop in front of their house. Daniel was in the back seat sitting next to Olivia. They exited the car as William and Natalie accompanied them.

Natalie said, "You must be Marilyn. I'm Natalie, and this is my husband, William, and our daughter, Olivia. We felt it was appropriate to introduce ourselves considering Daniel and Olivia are spending a lot of time together. He's joined us for dinner on a few occasions."

"That's very kind of you," Marilyn said with a smile. Her pleasant expression surprised Daniel. "Yes, they have been spending a lot of time together and now I can see why." Marilyn approached Olivia, knelt, and pinched her cheek. "You're beautiful." She stood up and was surprised when Natalie removed a glass dish from a bag.

She extended her arms and said, "I made you guys shepherd's pie. Daniel said it was Keith's favourite."

"You're too kind, but I can't accept—"

"We sure can!" Keith exclaimed, making his presence known. Daniel wrapped his arms around his father's legs.

Keith had surprised Marilyn. "What on earth are you doing out here? You should be in bed," she said.

"It's okay. I'm fine . . . and I actually have an appetite tonight," Keith said, laughing. "I heard a commotion and wanted to see what it was all about. Then I heard the name Olivia. Daniel talks about her all the time."

"Dad, stop," Daniel whined. Olivia smiled and nervously scrunched her shoulders.

"It's a pleasure to meet all of you, but I must get back inside. I look forward to enjoying some of that shepherd's pie."

Marilyn followed Keith inside after saying goodbye to the Roubles. Moments later, Daniel joined them at the table as Marilyn dispersed the food. Keith moaned in pleasure and said, "Seconds please."

After the introduction, Marilyn no longer questioned Daniel about his whereabouts, but never once did she apologize for the way she had treated him. Her focus, as Keith continued his chemotherapy, was on her liquor cabinet.

Halloween finally arrived and Daniel woke up early with a spring in his step. It was a Saturday, so not having to go to school added to his excitement. He grabbed his Dracula costume, tied the cape around his neck, placed a set of fangs in his mouth, and pranced around his room pretending to collect candy. He sang, "Trick or treat. Smell my feet. Give me something good to eat. If you don't, I don't care. I'll pull down your underwear."

Marilyn heard Daniel in his room. Nursing a hangover, she massaged her forehead, opened his door, and said, "Keep it down and take your costume off. We've got to take your dad to the hospital, remember?"

"Oh yeah! I forgot that today is his last round of chemo."

"That's right, and if it wasn't for you, he'd have an extra hour of sleep."

"Sorry."

"Not sorry enough, apparently. Now, get yourself ready and don't be late. If you're not outside in time, I'm leaving without you."

Daniel immediately took off his costume and changed into his blue jeans and a T-shirt that had a picture of Hulk Hogan on the front. He went to the bathroom, combed his hair, and brushed his teeth before heading to the kitchen. Daniel grabbed an apple and finished eating it on the porch. He heard the front door open just as he tossed the apple core into a nearby bush.

"Dad!"

Keith, upon noticing Daniel's T-shirt, began imitating Hulk Hogan and said, "Now, whatcha gonna do, brother, when the Hulkster comes for you?" He picked Daniel up and placed him on his knee. "Now, who's to say what will happen today, brother. But you can guarantee that I'm gonna lay the smackdown on some cancer today." Keith started tickling Daniel by poking his ribs. They laughed together. They both knew the effects of the chemotherapy treatments, but it was far from both of their minds.

That was, until Marilyn said, "Stop that, you two. Daniel, you should know better. Your dad is weak and can't play with you like that."

"It's all right. I feel good this morning."

"Well, you won't be saying that two hours from now."

"I'm not worried about two hours from now."

"You should be. You'll be spending the afternoon praying to the porcelain gods."

"Well, let's hope it's for the last time, eh?" Keith said as he smiled and winked at Daniel.

"Okay, then. Let's get going."

This was the first and only time Daniel had been invited to join his father for chemotherapy treatment. He had asked to come on previous occasions, but Keith felt it was inappropriate. However, seeing that this was a special circumstance, he looked forward to having Daniel by his side.

They were a few minutes from the hospital when Daniel asked, "Dad, are you going to be able to take me around trick-or-treating tonight?"

"Don't be silly, Daniel. Your father isn't going to have the energy," Marilyn said.

"Your mother's right. I expect to be bedridden the rest of the day."

"So . . . then, Mom, can you take me trick-or-treating?"

"Absolutely not. I have to look after your father. I won't even have time to answer the door or make jack-o-lanterns."

"Well, then who's going to take me?" Daniel whimpered.

"You cut that out right now, young man," Marilyn said.

Keith, wanting to defuse the increasing tension, said, "I had a chat with Olivia's parents the other day. They're going to take you around the neighbourhood."

"Really? And what about the old jailhouse to see Toothless Will?"

"Yep, they're going to take you there after some trick-or-treating."

Marilyn shrugged in relief as Daniel began singing to himself. Shortly after, they parked on the street outside the hospital and went inside. Keith, accustomed to the maze of hallways, escorted Marilyn and Daniel to the appropriate area and waited. Soon, a nurse, who congratulated Keith on his final round of treatment, took him and Daniel to a room filled with people in reclining chairs. Daniel sat on a stool and began to spin around while the nurse started the infusion. He watched in interest as his father relaxed in the recliner. With a smile on his face, Keith said, "Thank god this is the last time."

An hour later, he was done. Daniel had lost interest after the first ten minutes. They were both happy to be leaving and hoped that neither of them had to go back. They met Marilyn, who was sipping a cup of coffee in the waiting area. They shared a hug before getting into the car.

On the way home, Keith was already experiencing the side effects of the treatment. He held it together long enough to make it home, but as soon as he got inside, he made a beeline for the upstairs bathroom. The sound of him vomiting echoed throughout the house. He spent the remainder of the day in bed as Daniel played in his room. Marilyn poured herself a drink, sat on the front porch, and started smoking a cigarette.

Evening came quick enough, and it was accompanied by the sound of children scouring the neighbourhood to discuss who had more candy and which house handed out the full-size chocolate bars. The Roubles had already picked up Daniel and they, along with Olivia dressed as a witch, knocked on as many doors as they could. By the time the candles lighting the jack-o-lanterns were beginning to dim, Daniel and Olivia were waiting in line outside the old jail in downtown Port Dalhousie. It was a custom to visit the old jail on Halloween night because, according to legend, it was the only night when the ghost of Toothless Will visited the living. As the children entered, they were followed by screams of terror.

Daniel and Olivia were met at the entrance by an old man dressed as a pirate. He spoke in a rickety voice. "Only the bravest souls dare enter here. For it is only on Halloween night when the ghost of Toothless Will haunts the living. He's the only man who died of his crimes on this exact spot," he said, pointing to where Daniel and Olivia were standing. "Toothless Will was hanged. Some people say they can still hear his cries. Some people say they can hear his creepy, toothless laugh. Only the bravest enter here on Halloween night. Ye be warned."

Olivia took Daniel's hand and they looked at each other before entering the old jail. The door closed behind them, and they held their breath. It was completely dark. Only their increasing heartbeats could be heard. The smell of cobwebs, dust, and century-old wood filled their noses. Olivia gasped upon hearing a chain being dragged. Daniel, trying to prove his manliness, walked in front toward the far door. He stopped when he heard someone laughing.

Terrified, they clung to each other as the door nearest to them opened. The sound of a wooden box falling spooked them. They turned around and, as light shone in from the door behind them, they saw Toothless Will standing in the far corner with a noose hanging around his neck. He was wearing torn clothing, and he had a long beard and a patch over his left eye. Toothless Will laughed and lunged at Daniel and Olivia. They screamed and started running toward the open door. Toothless Will chased them out of the jail and before closing the door, he said, "I'll remember you two, Daniel and Olivia."

27

Astonished, they ran to where William and Natalie were waiting. Still shaking, they looked at each other before saying in unison, "He knows our names!"

Their excitement continued as they tried their best to illustrate what happened. However, the only thing William and Natalie could do was nod in agreement even though they could not understand what the kids were saying. They reminisced about their experience the entire walk back to Daniel's house. Marilyn was waiting on the porch. She stood unsteadily and slurred her speech when she said, "So good to see that everyone made it home safely."

William approached and was close enough to smell the alcohol on her breath. "Yes, we had a great time this Halloween," he said.

"Our first Halloween in Port Dalhousie. Look!" Olivia said as she opened her bag of treats.

"They sure put on a good show down at Lakeside Park, don't they, Marilyn?" Natalie said.

"Fantastic. Well, time for Daniel to go to bed. Have a good night," Marilyn said as she stumbled toward the door.

"Good night," the Roubles said in unison.

Olivia gave Daniel a hug and a kiss on the cheek before leaving. To him, that was better than all the contents in his Halloween bag. He followed his mother inside and said, "Mom, you will not believe what happened tonight. We got a boatload of candy. Then, we went down to the old jail to see Toothless Will and—"

"I don't really care, Daniel. Just go to bed, would ya. If it makes you happy, you can eat all the candy you want. Just don't bother me, okay. I'm tired."

Daniel frowned and made his way upstairs. He kept his head down. He passed by his parents' room and noticed the door was open. He looked inside, hoping his father would be excited to hear the news, but there was no one in the room. He yelled from the top of the stairs, "Where's Dad?"

"Oh shhhh ... Ahhh ... He had to go back to the hospital. Uhhh ... He forgot his wallet. Now, go to bed!"

"When will he be back?"

"Daniel, that's enough! Go to bed!"

Deflated once again, Daniel went to his room, closed the door, and emptied the contents of his bag on the floor. He was sorting his candy into different piles when he heard his father's car pull into the driveway. He squinted to get a better look and noticed that Keith was carrying a large garbage bag underneath his arm. Wanting to question his father, Daniel hurriedly made his way downstairs. However, Marilyn could hear his footsteps and by the time he was midway to the door, she exclaimed, "Daniel. If you take one more step, I'm gonna throw out all of your candy. Now, go to bed!"

Daniel, for the third time since being home, finally succumbed to his mother's demands. He locked himself in his room and heard his father enter the house. "I'm exhausted. I need to go to bed," Keith said. Daniel heard his feet shuffling up the stairs. He hoped his father would knock on his door, but there was nothing. Moments later, he heard his mother pour herself another drink. She turned on the evening news and remained slumped on the couch. Daniel cried himself to sleep.

# CHAPTER FOUR

## Peanut Butter Pete

The following summer, one day after Daniel's eighth birthday, Marilyn found her son playing on the front porch with his new He-Man action figures. He was about to defeat Skeletor with a thrust of his sword, but his movement was stopped when Megatron came swooping down and blasted He-Man into oblivion. Then, out of nowhere, Hulk Hogan jumped off the railing and smashed Megatron into pieces.

"Take that, Megatron!" Daniel said, trying to sound like Hulk Hogan. "Bonk, bonk, bonk. You're next, Skeletor. I don't think so!" he said. Now imitating Skeletor: "Take that! And that! Bwahaha! You're dead!"

"Daniel, what is all that noise?" Marilyn said.

Daniel jolted upon hearing her voice. "S-sorry, Mom."

"Not sorry enough! I already told you your father was resting. He's doing better, but the party took a lot out of him yesterday."

"But I'm so bored. Will you play with me, Mom?"

"Daniel, are you stupid? After everything I did yesterday to make sure your birthday party went off without a hitch, the only thing I want to do today is recuperate."

"What should I do?"

"Well . . . take your bike somewhere. School is over. Go play with your friends or go over to Olivia's place," Marilyn said as she threw her hands up. "I don't care where you go as long as it's not here."

"Fine," Daniel complained as he scrunched his eyebrows and dropped his new toys.

"You better not give me any attitude, young man. Especially after everything I did for you yesterday. Any more of that and you'll be spending the rest of the day in your room."

Daniel stomped his way into the house. He changed out of his pyjamas and put on his new G.I. Joe T-shirt. He could hear his father snoring as he made his way downstairs. He was about to leave when Marilyn said, "Better take some food with you. There's lots of leftovers from the party yesterday. You better eat 'em up because I'll be darned if I'm going to throw good food into the garbage."

Daniel grabbed his backpack and loaded it with triangle-shaped peanut butter and jam sandwiches, sliced carrots, cheese, and brownies. He put on a brand-new pair of sneakers, jumped down the porch stairs, and took his bike from the garage. He took his mother's advice and started pedalling his way toward Olivia's house when there was a familiar noise in the distance. Already several blocks away from home, Daniel came to a stop as the noise got closer. It was too late by the time he recognized what and who it was coming from.

"Is that Daniel freaking Harris?" said Josh Thompson as he skidded the rear tire of his bike. He stopped a few inches in front of Daniel, blocking his way. He was accompanied by two other boys. They were just as dirty as Josh was. Their clothing had holes along the seams, and they had short, greasy hair. Their gaze intimidated Daniel.

"Oh . . . hey, Josh. How ya doin?" Daniel said nervously.

"Just look at me . . . I'm fantastic. These are the Goodwin twins, Gary and Tom."

"Sup," they responded in unison. Daniel could not tell the difference between them except that Tom had a scar on his chin and was several inches taller.

"Nice shoes," Gary said, "Check 'em out, Tom."

"Whoa, nice kicks, bro. Can I try 'em on?" Tom asked.

"Uh . . . I just got these for my birthday," Daniel said as he slowly backed away.

"Oh, come on, man. I just wanna try 'em on."

Daniel took another step back. Josh and Gary began to laugh.

Tom grabbed Daniel's arm and said, "Grab 'em!"

The three rebels picked up Daniel off his bike and threw him, facedown, onto the grassy boulevard. Josh sat on his back as Gary held his legs together. Tom removed his new sneakers as Daniel tried to thrash around. They began shouting in excitement as Daniel watched. He looked at his exposed socks and began to cry.

"Oh, come on, you wuss. I was just kidding," Tom said.

"Yeah, ya wuss," Gary added.

"Here ya go, Dan. You can have your shoes back, but only if you stop crying," Josh said.

Daniel wiped the tears from his eyes, grabbed his grass-stained shoes, and said, "Why did you do that?"

"Oh relax, Dan. We were just Joshin' you around," Tom said.

"Yeah, just Joshin' you. Relax," Gary added.

Josh extended his hand and pulled Daniel to his feet. Daniel removed his backpack to see if any of its squished contents were salvageable.

"You had brownies and you didn't even tell us? Give me one," Tom demanded.

"I want one too!" Gary said.

Daniel reluctantly gave them a brownie each. Josh took his backpack and began rummaging through the remainder.

"Hey, that's my stuff," Daniel cried.

"Oh, don't worry, Dan. I'm just lookin'," Josh said as he threw the bags of carrots and cheese on the ground. "You have peanut butter and jam sandwiches in here?"

"Yeah."

"You know what we should do, guys? We should go see Peanut Butter Pete."

"Awesome idea!" Tom said.

"Yeah, awesome. He'll do anything for a peanut butter sandwich," Gary added.

"Who's Peanut Butter Pete?" Daniel asked as he picked up the strewn bags.

"Follow us," Josh commanded as he returned Daniel's backpack.

The three friends grabbed their bikes and began pedalling away from Daniel in the opposite direction from Olivia's house. Reluctantly, Daniel followed them. They continued their excursion farther across the city than Daniel had ever been. They passed the Fairview mall and followed the path along the old Welland Canal system. With each push of his pedals, Daniel was becoming more confused about his surroundings. They continued heading north and stopped at the entrance to a park that Daniel had never seen before.

"Where are we?" he asked.

"Royal Henley Park. What, you never been here before?" Josh scoffed.

"I have no idea where I am."

"Oh boy, you need to get out more, Dan. Come on . . ."

"Peanut Butter Pete usually sets up his tent over here," Tom said, pointing to a set of massive maple trees situated along the top of the old canal. Daniel approached the edge and nearly lost his nerve as he looked down to see a sunken ship in murky water. It was a thirty-foot drop. He began to back up when Josh grabbed his body and yelled, "Gotcha!"

Josh pretended that he was going to throw Daniel over the edge but stopped when Gary said, "We found Peanut Butter Pete."

Daniel followed Josh and watched as he, Tom, and Gary approached a yellow-and-blue tent nestled underneath a large bush. They started mocking the person inside, saying, "Peanut Butter Pete, where are you? You look like a bum and smell like poo."

The opening of the tent was undone, and Daniel could see a man lying inside. He sat up and had dirt across his forehead. His hair was messy as he scratched his thick, dirty beard.

"Get the hell outta here, you punks! If ya knew what was good for you," he said in a rough voice.

"We have something for ya, Peanut Butter Pete," Josh said as he held up a plastic bag that contained a section of Daniel's sandwich.

"Is that peanut butter?" Pete asked as he emerged from his tent. He stood up straight and was over six feet tall.

"And strawberry jam," Gary added.

"Well, what are you waiting for?"

"You want it?

"Yeah."

"Bark like a dog and I'll give it to ya," Josh said as he, Tom, and Gary laughed.

Pete noticed Daniel was not laughing and stared at him for a short while. "You look familiar, kid."

"Ah, shut up, Pete," Josh said as he raised the bag higher. "Now, bark like a dog and I'll give you this sandwich."

To Daniel's surprise, Peanut Butter Pete started barking and panting like a dog. Josh, Gary, and Tom joined in. The continued to laugh until Pete playfully lunged at Josh, scaring him so he dropped the bag containing the sandwich. Pete picked it up and started barking again as he went inside his tent. "Now, get the hell outta here, ya punks."

"Let's go swimming!" Tom said.

"Yeah, swimming," Gary added.

"C'mon, Dan. There's a great spot to jump off over here," Josh said as he followed Tom and Gary down a path leading beyond the sunken ship.

Daniel hesitated. He wanted to leave and go home but had no idea where he was.

"Is your last name Harris?" asked Pete. Daniel had not noticed he was standing behind him.

"Ya . . . yes. My name is Daniel Harris."

"Is your father Keith Harris?"

"Yes."

"He still a cop?"

"Uh huh."

"Yeah, I know your dad. Great guy . . . always nice to me. So, what the heck are you doin' hangin' around those guys anyway? You seem like a nice kid."

Daniel did not know what to say, but he began to feel comfortable around Pete the longer he spoke.

"Do you have any more peanut butter sandwiches?" Pete asked.

Daniel opened his backpack and produced three more bags. He gave them to Pete and said, "Don't worry. I won't make you bark like a dog."

"Oh, I don't care about that. Say, how's your dad doing anyway? I heard he has cancer, is that right?"

"Yeah . . . had cancer."

"Is that right. He still alive?"

"Yeah."

"Good for him. No wonder I haven't seen him around. I could really go for a quarter-pounder right about now."

"How did you know he had cancer?"

"Me and your dad go way back. He used to check in on me from time to time, usually brings me McDonald's. I used to stay at the shelter next to the YMCA on King Street, but I got harassed too much there and my stuff was always being stolen. So, I came here about two years ago. Loved it ever since. Fresh air, lots of space. No one bothers me, except for when your buddy Josh is in the park."

"Yeah, he can be a troublemaker. My mom told me he's a bad influence, but my dad always gave him a chance."

"He would. Your dad's a good guy. I miss him a lot. You let him know I say hi and hope to see him around sometime. Thanks for the sandwiches."

"Okay," Daniel said, still trying to grasp the conversation and how Peanut Butter Pete knew his father. Moments later, he heard Josh calling his name. He followed the sound of his voice.

Pete remained nestled underneath a large maple tree, eating the sandwiches Daniel gave him. He watched as Daniel, Josh, Tom, and Gary took off their shirts and, one by one, jumped off the top of the thirty-foot-high barrier and into the water below.

Intimidated by the height, Daniel hesitated to jump and remained at the top of the old canal. Tom, Gary, and Josh were taunting him from below and threatened that if he did not jump by the time they got to the top, they would throw him in. Daniel tried to gather the courage to jump but his nerves got the better of him. The boys hurried up the embankment, grabbed Daniel by his arms and legs, and began swinging him like a pendulum.

"On three!" Josh yelled.

Daniel screamed and tried to loosen their grip, but he could not get free.

"One . . . two . . . three!" they counted and threw Daniel over the edge. They did not throw him far enough, and the back of his head caught the edge of the cement barrier. The force of the blow knocked Daniel unconscious and his limp body plummeted toward the water. Tom, Gary, and Josh watched in stunned silence as Daniel's body slapped against the surface of the water. His body did not move. He slowly began to sink, but then, suddenly, there was a grunt followed by a large splash.

"Is that . . ." Josh said.

"It's Peanut Butter Pete! Let's get outta here!" Tom said.

"Yeah, let's get outta here," Gary echoed.

Josh, the only one of the three who hesitated, eventually followed his friends after watching Pete carry Daniel's limp body to the edge of the embankment.

"Help! Help! Call an ambulance!" Pete cried.

Bystanders came running. They watched as Pete held Daniel in his arms. Daniel was breathing but still unconscious; blood was pouring from a cut on the back of his head. Several tense minutes passed until the police arrived. They took Daniel to a waiting ambulance and sped off toward the hospital.

The next thing Daniel remembered was waking up in the hospital. Bright fluorescent lights hindered his sight, but he was able to discern who was in the room based on the sound of their voice.

"He's awake!"

"Mom? Is that you?"

"Yes, my dear. Oh my god, we were so worried about you," Marilyn said as she gave Daniel a hug. The display of emotion was a surprise to him. It was comforting, and he enjoyed the moment as he listened to his mother's beating heart, encompassed by her warmth.

"How are you doing, Daniel?" Keith asked as he entered the room.

"My head hurts," he said, gingerly touching the back of his skull.

"Don't touch your stitches," Marilyn said as she grabbed his hand.

"Stiches?"

"Eighteen stiches to be exact," said a doctor as he entered the room. He was tall and slim. He had smile on his face and Daniel noticed his perfectly combed silver hair. "I'm Dr. Fitzgerald, but you can call me Fitzy. Do you remember what happened, Daniel?"

"No."

As Dr. Fitzgerald described Daniel's traumatic adventure at Royal Henley Park, Keith remained at the end of the bed with his arms crossed. Marilyn sunk into a chair and began grinding her teeth as the details were presented.

"Who is this Pete person you're talking about?" Marilyn asked.

"Peanut Butter Pete, Dr. Fitzgerald?" Keith commented.

"Yes. Peanut Butter Pete saved Daniel's life."

"The hobo!" Marilyn exclaimed. "He probably pushed Daniel over the edge."

"Hey! I know Pete. He'd never do that," Keith said.

"Actually, Pete told me it was Josh Thompson and the Goodwin twins," Dr. Fitzgerald said.

"He's right," Daniel added, slowly beginning to remember the details of what happened. "They threw me over the edge and that's when I hit my head."

"Josh Thompson! The Goodwin twins! What the hell were you doing with them? You were supposed to be at the Roubles'," Marilyn said.

Wanting to defuse the tension, Dr. Fitzgerald said, "Daniel's okay to go home now. Remember that he's had a traumatic day. Give him some Tylenol before bed and tomorrow as needed. I'll see you in two weeks to have the stitches removed."

Marilyn did her best to remain calm, but it only lasted until they got home. She went immediately to the kitchen and poured herself a drink.

"I'll go pick up pizza and wings from the Kilt. Be back in thirty," Keith said.

"See you . . . in thirty," Marilyn responded in between sips.

"Can I go with you, Dad?" Daniel pleaded.

"Better not, son. You need to rest."

Daniel was desperate to be somewhere other than the confines of the house with his mother. His anxieties about her anger were valid, and when the door closed, his assumptions turned to reality.

Marilyn stormed down the hallway, grabbed Daniel by the neck, and forced him in front of the bathroom mirror. She said, "Tell me what you see!"

Daniel did not respond. He looked at the floor instead.

"Look at yourself! I'll tell you what I see. I see a liar. I see a punk kid that tried to kill his mother with worry. Do you have any idea what I went through today?"

Marilyn's barrage continued for several minutes. Daniel, knowing the best thing to do was to not say anything, stared into the mirror and began to believe everything his mother was saying. *Maybe I am a liar. Maybe I am a punk. Maybe I am a loser,* he thought.

Once finished and out of breath, Marilyn slapped him on the side of the head and yelled, "Now, go to your room!" She went back to the kitchen and refilled her glass as Daniel cried under his sheets. With red eyes, he looked out his window and hoped his father would be back soon.

Ten minutes later, once Daniel had cried himself out, Keith arrived holding a fresh pizza and a pound of steaming chicken wings. Daniel came running down the stairs and hugged his father. He grimaced upon smelling the spice on the chicken wings.

"Are you okay, son? It looks like you've been crying," Keith said.

Daniel, seeing the dangerous look from his mother, said, "I'm fine."

"Okay. Must be the chicken wings then. They are spicy! Who's hungry?

# CHAPTER FIVE

## First Impressions

The next four years were good to the Harris family. Keith recovered from his chemotherapy treatment and his cancer was in complete remission. He had the strength to play catch with Daniel and chase him around the yard again. As a family, they would often go for bike rides to the pier and watch the sunset. Marilyn's smile returned and every chance she could steal a kiss with Keith, she would. Keith went back to work and those in the neighbourhood were happy to see him cruising around in his police car. With renewed sense of purpose, he took advantage of every waking hour. His constant smile was accompanied by a positive attitude and his energy was an encouraging influence on Daniel.

Keith had a heightened understanding of life and how fragile it can be. He used his acceptance of his own mortality to pursue interests he had once set aside like ping pong and golf. Keith did not waste the opportunity to advise Daniel on the peculiarities of life. He sought to teach Daniel the many lessons he had learned while spending countless hours lying in bed. The most important lesson he learned was forgiveness. "Forgiveness, like anything else, requires practice," he would tell Daniel frequently, "and the more you practice forgiveness, the better you get at it. Once the ability to offer it becomes natural, it allows you to live life without the burden of hatred, shame, or regret."

Recently, the focus of Keith's forgiveness was toward his older brother, Ross. His wanting to express it was the reason for the excursion he and Daniel were about to embark on.

There was a knock at Daniel's door. He opened his eyes and noticed his room was completely dark. He heard his door creak open as Keith whispered, "Rise and shine. We've got a big day ahead of us."

"Oh, Dad," Daniel whined, "why do we have to get up so early?"

Keith sat next to him and scratched his back. "Because we've got a five-hour drive ahead of us."

"Oh man. Do I really have to go?" Daniel said as he pulled the blanket over his shoulder.

"Fine, you can stay home."

"Really?"

"But it would be just you and your mother for seven days."

"Never mind. I'm ready," Daniel said as he kicked the blanket off the bed and rolled out of bed.

"Thought so." Keith chuckled.

After getting dressed, Daniel quietly made his way downstairs and placed his duffel bag by the front door. His smelled bacon and scrambled eggs, and he tripped over his bag trying to get to the food, landing with a thud on the hallway floor. Daniel held his breath and remained motionless.

"Oh, for the love of . . ." Marilyn said from the bedroom. She made her way to the top of the stairs. "Did you forget how to walk, Daniel?"

"Sorry, Mom."

"Not sorry enough."

"Why don't you go back to sleep?"

"Once I'm up, I'm up. And I can smell coffee," Marilyn said as she walked past Daniel. "Of all the days I get woken up . . . on the weekend when I get to sleep in."

Keith, unaware of what was happening because he was busy making breakfast, was surprised to see Marilyn sitting at the kitchen table. She sat slumped over with her elbow on the table, her hand propping up her head. Her hair looked like a rat's nest and her nightgown was wrinkled.

"Still not a morning person, eh, hon?"

"Never."

Keith poured Marilyn a cup of coffee. She grasped the mug with both hands and brought it to her mouth and sipped. Relishing in the warmth, Marilyn smiled and said, "I love coffee." Daniel sat next to her and ate his breakfast.

"Well, at least I get a break from both of ya for the next week," Marilyn said. "God knows I've earned it."

"Do you have any plans while we're away?"

"Yeah . . . relax and see if I can get these grey hairs to turn brown again." She laughed. "No big plans. Go see my parents. My dad got a new shipment of Scotch he wants to try."

"Oh my," Keith said as he rolled his eyes. "You know what happens when your family gets into the sauce."

"Yep, and we're not going to change for anything," Marilyn said. "Speaking of family, how long has it been since you've seen Ross?"

"Uh . . . seven years. It was just after Daniel was born."

"Why so long?" Daniel asked.

Marilyn leaned toward his ear and said, "He's a little weird."

"No, he's not," Keith said.

"He's a hippie, and he smokes weed. Makes him paranoid."

"He smokes weeds?" Daniel said, tilting his head.

"Marijuana," Keith responded. "He's been smoking it for years."

"You know, Daniel, that your father arrests people for having it."

"Really? Did you arrest Uncle Ross?"

Keith excused himself to the bathroom and said, "No, I never arrested Uncle Ross."

Marilyn, upon finishing her cup of coffee, added, "He's a homosexual, too. He and his Indian buddy, Wade."

"Homo . . . sexual?" Daniel asked as he raised an eyebrow.

"You know how you like Olivia?"

"Yeah."

"Well, your Uncle Ross likes other men the way you like Olivia."

"Really? That's gross."

"You're darn tootin', it's gross. And don't get suckered into listening to one of his Indian friend's stories. He'll go on and on about this and that and before you know it, he's askin' you for money so he can go buy booze and get drunk with all his Indian friends. Then he'll start whining about how the white man took his land and all that B.S.," whispered Marilyn, but she stopped when Keith came back into the kitchen.

They finished breakfast as a family. Soon after, Keith loaded the car, and they were on their way. Marilyn remained on the porch and waved until they were out of sight.

It turned out to be a beautiful morning. There was a cloudless sky as they got on the highway. Daniel remained transfixed on the countryside and watched as kilometre after kilometre of trees, vineyards, fruit, and dairy farms rolled past. Keith moved to the outer lane as they approached the Burlington skyway. The tires made a thump, thump sound after crossing each section of the bridge. Daniel could see all of Lake Ontario and was amazed at how big and blue it was.

They remained on the 401 through Toronto. Keith pointed to the CN tower and said, "So, you see that big hole in the ground next to it? That's going to be a new stadium for the Blue Jays. It's going to be called the Skydome. Pretty awesome, eh?"

Daniel continued to look in wonder as massive skyscrapers passed his window. Toronto eventually vanished beyond the horizon as they continued past Ajax, Oshawa, and Belleville. They turned north onto Highway 62 after stopping for some gas and a snack. Daniel continued to look out with wonder as endless acres of trees and lakes went by; he had not witnessed anything so beautiful.

He knew they were getting close when he noticed the sign welcoming them to Algonquin National Park. Daniel, happy knowing that the drive was coming to an end, rolled down his window and took a deep breath. The air was fresh, and he could smell the scent of pine trees and lake water. They continued down a gravel road and stopped in front of a cabin made of wood.

Keith honked the horn twice. A man poked his head out from behind the front door and smiled. He jogged toward the car with open arms. "You little rascal!" Uncle Ross laughed. "Get over here, little brother. It's been so long. Let me have a look atcha. You look good."

"Thanks. I feel good."

"I'm so glad you and Daniel are able to join us. It's too bad that Marilyn couldn't make it."

"Yeah, well you know how she is in nature."

"Like oil and water," Ross laughed as he and Keith embraced.

Daniel noticed subtle differences between the two. They had the same facial features, but Ross was several inches taller. He had a long beard and the hair on the top of his head was thinning.

Another man was standing behind them. He had dark skin and black braided hair that went down to his waist. He was intimidatingly tall and was wearing blue jeans, thick boots, and a long-sleeved plaid shirt. He smiled and walked toward Daniel with open arms. Daniel, however, kept his arms by his side. "And this must be Daniel. I haven't seen you since you were this big," he said, spreading his hands apart to show Daniel how small he had been. "It's so good to see you. I can't wait to show you and your dad around Algonquin Park."

"Hi, Wade," Keith said.

"Get over here, man," Wade exclaimed as Keith extended his hand. "No, we hug around here."

Wade picked up Daniel with one arm and put his other arm around Keith's shoulders. Wade squeezed so hard that they groaned. Daniel's nose twitched. "I smell something weird. It smells like a skunk," he said.

The three adults looked at each other with raised eyebrows. Then Ross laughed and said, "Lots of those around here. Now, get over here and give me a hug."

When Daniel hugged Ross, he smelled the same odour that emanated from Wade's clothing. Assuming it was caused by the same skunk, he quickly disregarded it and started unloading the car. Ross and Wade continued to talk as they escorted their guests to a nearby one-room cabin. They went inside and threw their belongings on the floor; the smell of cedar and smoky embers cooling in the fireplace engulfed them. At the front of the cabin was a large window that overlooked a lake. Daniel was awestruck by the beauty of nature.

"That's Lake Opeongo. You guys wanna go for a swim?" Wade asked.

"Please, Dad!" Daniel whined.

"That's why we came here, isn't it?" Keith said.

"We'll meet you at the beach in ten," Ross said, and he and Wade gave them another hug before leaving.

Daniel changed and waited for his father on the porch. He sat in a rocking chair and thought about his mother. Wade and Ross were completely different than what Marilyn told him to expect. They were happy and excited to be hosting Daniel and his father. Daniel felt comfortable here and was excited to be around them.

"Ready?" Keith asked, wearing his blue-and-red swim trunks, his yellow towel hanging around his neck. They walked down a gravel path toward the beach.

"What was Mom talking about when she told me Wade whined a lot and asked for money to buy booze?" Daniel asked.

Keith shrugged and said, "Your mother has a—let's say . . . a tainted view of the Native people of Canada."

"What's a Native? I think Mom calls them Indians."

"Ah . . . that's not really the most appropriate thing to call them. You see, Wade's ancestors were here for thousands of years before us. This land belongs to them and it was taken away."

"Who took it?"

"We did."

"We did?"

"Well, our great-great-great-great-grandfathers did."

"Why?"

"Ah . . . that's a loaded question, Daniel. I'm not sure I'm the best person to tell you why. Wade would know more about that. You can ask him later if you'd like," Keith said, rubbing the back of his neck.

Silence between them remained as they approached the beach. Keith removed his shirt, turned to look at Daniel, and asked, "Well, what are you waiting for? Take your shirt off and jump in."

Daniel crossed his arms and with a confused look said, "Mom also told me to watch out because Uncle Ross is a homo."

Keith's eyes widened and his mouth was agape. "I think I need to speak with your mother when we get home."

"She told me he likes men and that I should watch myself when I'm around both of them."

"Oh my . . ." Keith said as he motioned for Daniel to sit next to him. "There's no need to be afraid of Uncle Ross or Wade. Yes, they are in a relationship, but the feelings they have for each other are no different than the way I feel about your mother. And just as there are men who like other men, there are women who like other women."

"Really?"

"Yes, and there's no need to fear them either."

"But they're different."

"Just because they're different doesn't mean that you should be afraid of them. Your Uncle Ross and Wade love you for who you are. Should you not love them for who they are?" Keith said as he stood up to greet his brother.

"Last one in is a smelly pig!" Wade exclaimed as he ran into the water. He was quickly joined by Ross and Keith. Daniel watched as they splashed each other and thought about what his father said. Moments later, he removed his shirt and swam out to join them. Each one took turns thrusting Daniel into the air and laughed as he came down with a splash; a competition between who could toss him higher ensued. They swam out to a floating dock that had a diving board. They each took turns making silly movements in the air and trying to make the biggest splash.

Keith was the first to retire. He rested on the side of the dock and coughed. It was not noticeable enough to be a concern, but it did provide Keith with a reason to excuse himself to relax on the beach. From there, he watched Daniel, Ross, and Wade continue their antics until they, too, were exhausted from the afternoon's activities. They went back to their cabins and changed. Soon after, there was a knock on the door.

"Hi, Wade," Keith said.

"I'm about to go catch some dinner. Would you guys like to come?"

"Ah . . . I'm pretty tired."

"I wanna go!" Daniel yelled.

"Okay, but you have to wear a life jacket."

"Yes!"

"We're going to take that boat right there," Wade said as he pointed to the nearest dock. Daniel started running toward it. He put on an orange life jacket and waved at his father.

Keith waved back and said to Wade, "Would you do me a favour?"

"Sure, whatever you need."

"I'm concerned about Daniel. He keeps to himself more than usual. I've tried talking to him, but he won't open up to me so . . ."

"I understand," Wade said as he winked.

"Thanks," Keith said as he closed the door and rested on the couch; a nagging cough kept him awake.

Daniel jumped in the boat and sat nearest the bow as Wade started the engine. They pulled away quickly and began skipping across the water. Daniel peered over the edge and watched as the disturbed water made ripples behind them. He closed his eyes and enjoyed the sensation of the wind on his face. They continued around a bend and were beyond the sight of the cabins when they stopped. Daniel noticed fallen trees underneath the water and thick grass growing along the shore. The water was calm and peaceful. There was no wind, and the water reflected the blue sky as the setting sun exposed a cascade of colours across the clouds.

"This is my favourite fishing hole, Daniel. Not yet have I gone home empty handed. Trout, bass, pike . . . you name it, I've caught it right here. Have you ever fished before?" Wade asked as he prepared a fishing pole. Daniel watched as he attached a lure.

"No."

"Never? Well, there's a first time for everything. Here, you can have this one. It's my lucky rod."

Daniel accepted his offer, but the handle got twisted in his shirt. "How do I . . . uh . . ."

"Watch me," Wade said as he pressed a button on the reel and flicked his wrist forward. Daniel watched as his lure made a splash twenty feet away from the boat. "And then you start reeling it in like this. Hopefully, there will be a fish on the end soon."

Daniel emulated Wade, and after a few attempts he was casting his lure just as far. He experienced a sense of pride as he watched it splash into the water. He did not have to wait long until he felt a tug.

"That's it, Daniel. Now, pull the rod up, and keep reeling like this," Wade said as he hung a large net over the side of the boat. "Almost there . . . got it! Holy cow, it's a whopper!"

Daniel laughed but his happiness turned to anxiety as Wade took the fish out of the net and placed it on the bottom of the boat. The fish flapped and jumped around, scaring Daniel. He quickly raised his feet and grasped the frame of the boat. However, as the display subsided, he regained composure and noticed Wade smiling at him. Wade placed the fish in a large box and covered it in ice. "That should feed the four of us. Want to help me prepare the fish?"

"Prepare the fish?" Daniel said as he gulped. "Sure . . ."

"That's the spirit. Now, let's go," Wade said as he tried to start the engine, but it did not turn over. He tried several more times, but nothing happened. "Huh . . . Looks like we'll have to paddle back. You take that one and I'll take this one."

Daniel grabbed the oar nearest to him, sat next to Wade, and began to mimic him. It was not long until they got into a rhythm, and they found themselves making progress. They were rounding the bend when Wade asked, "So, how's it going, Daniel?"

"Good."

"Is there anything you want to talk about?"

"Um . . . I don't know."

"Well, are you happy that your dad beat cancer?"

"Yeah."

"And what about your mom? Is she happy?"

"I don't know. I don't care, really."

"Why not?"

"Because she called me names and made me feel bad. She yelled at me and made me stand in front of the mirror for a long time and said things like 'You're a liar' and 'You're the reason why I drink.'"

Wade stopped rowing for a moment and asked, "How did that make you feel?"

"Angry and frustrated. I hated my mom when she was doing that stuff to me."

"And how do you feel about your mother now?"

"I haven't really thought about it," Daniel said as he continued to row. Wade suggested they take a break to catch their breath. Daniel watched the water dripping off the end of the oar, the drops creating ripples on the surface of the water. "She's been happier since my dad got better. She doesn't pick on me as much, but she still gets angry and yells at me sometimes. She says some mean things, but I just don't pay attention anymore."

Wade took a deep breath and waited a moment to respond before asking, "Why do you think she said those things to you?"

"I don't know. Because she's angry. She used to always tell me how stressed she was."

"Yes, stress is powerful, and it has had a profound effect on your mother."

"What do you mean?"

"Well, stress is a primal response to your surroundings. It evolved as a survival mechanism and it causes one of two things, Daniel. Have you heard of the term 'fight or flight'?"

"No."

"Well, can you remember a time when you were really scared?"

"Yeah. I wanted to run but my friends grabbed me and threw me into the canal," Daniel said as he rubbed the scar on the back of his head.

"Yes, I heard about that," Wade said as he continued to row. "So, your reaction was to run, or flight, but your mom's instinctive reaction is to fight when confronted by stress. She gets angry and yells and has no control over her reactions, is that right?"

"Yes."

"This might be difficult to accept, but when your mom is acting like that, yelling at you and calling you names, try not to take it personally. Because it has nothing to do with you and it has everything to do with your mother and how her brain is biologically reacting to stress."

"I don't understand." Daniel sighed.

"Well, did you ever consider that your mom did those things because she's scared?"

"Scared! Scared of what?"

"Losing your father. I'm sure she had a lot on her mind about what life would be like if your dad had died. It's scary to think about that kind of stuff. I'm sure she loves your dad and watching him go through chemotherapy was distressing for her."

"I never thought about it that way before. And what about her drinking? She drinks all the time now," Daniel added.

"Well, sometimes things like alcohol can be a coping mechanism for people dealing with their own feelings."

"What's a coping mech-a . . ."

"Nism. Mechanism. Um . . . how did you deal with the bad news that your dad had cancer? What did you do to help make it through?"

Daniel paused for a while and thought about what helped him. "Olivia," he said and smiled. "I would play with my friend Olivia and that would make me feel better."

"Well, alcohol makes your mom feel better the same way that Olivia made you feel better. Is she your girlfriend?"

"Ew . . . nope."

"Well, do you like her?"

"Uh . . . yes."

"Have you told her you like her?"

"No way!"

Wade laughed. He looked over his shoulder and noticed they were a few minutes away from the dock. "Can I tell you a story my dad once told me? It has been passed on in my family for generations. It's about a flower that wouldn't open its petals. Would you like to hear it?"

"Sure."

"A long time ago when the earth was new and there was an abundance of life, there was a single, lonely flower in the middle of a massive field. One day, a bee came along and began climbing its stem. The bee asked the flower if it could open its petals so it could get to the pollen, but the flower refused because it was afraid to get stung. Day after day, the bee came back and every time he asked for pollen, the flower remained closed. Eventually, the flower got sick because it was sad. It started to wilt, and it no longer had the strength to keep itself closed. Taking advantage of the weakened flower, the stubborn bee snuck inside and began collecting all the pollen it could carry. It would fly home every night and come back every day. Several days passed, and the flower began to get better. She knew it was because of the bee that she was improving. After that, the flower remained open whenever the bee came by and, before long, they became friends. Months passed, and as the bee spread the pollen throughout the field, hundreds of flowers began to grow and the once sad, lonesome flower wasn't sad and alone anymore."

Daniel scrunched his face and said, "I don't get it."

By the time Wade had finished his story, they were arriving at the dock nearest to their cabin. Keith met them and secured the boat to the dock. Wade smiled and winked at Keith as he carried the large cooler to a nearby picnic table. He took out the fish and removed a knife from his pocket. Daniel, excited to show his father the fish he caught, took Keith's hand, and pulled him to where Wade was. Keith shared in Daniel's delight and was happy to see how excited he was.

"Daniel is going to help prepare the fish he caught," Wade said.

"Great! I'll help Ross get the fire going."

Keith joined his older brother, and they began reminiscing about days of old as the wood became engulfed in flame. Consumed with laughter, Ross said, "And do you remember when Dad used to sit in his recliner after dinner?"

"Oh yeah, and he would rub his belly until he would burp."

"I remember playing crokinole after dinner until our knuckles hurt."

"Yeah, but do you remember we used to play by lying on the floor?"

"Oh yeah . . . because Dad's farts smelled so bad!"

"And do you remember what Mom used to say?"

Ross and Keith resumed their conversation, and their laughter echoed across the lake. Daniel smiled at Wade as he hovered his hands above the fish. He was murmuring some words that Daniel could not understand. "What are you doing?" Daniel asked.

"It's a post-kill ritual that my people have done for generations. I'm appreciating the fish and the sacrifice it made. It died so that we may live."

"Huh. Is that your knife? It's really cool."

"Yeah, the handle is made from elk horn. I made the blade myself."

"What's that?" Daniel asked, pointing to a design on the side of the knife.

"That's my spirit animal. It's a wolf."

"Cool."

Daniel was intrigued as he watched Wade remove the meat from the fish. He put the contents into the cooler and tossed the fish carcass into the water.

"So, what do you think about the story between the flower and the bee?" Wade asked as he rinsed his hands.

"Oh, I don't know."

"Well, which one are you? The flower or the bee?"

Daniel took a moment before responding, "The bee."

"That's right, and who is the flower?"

"Uh, my mom."

"That's right. Do you remember what made the flower better? It was the love and stubbornness of the bee. Maybe your mom needs to be reminded that you love her. Maybe your mom needs your support to help get through tough times, too."

"I don't know."

"Will you try something when you go home in a few days?"

"Sure."

"Give your mom a hug and tell you that you love her and see what happens. Promise?

"Promise."

Wade and Daniel joined Keith and Ross. They enjoyed dinner as the raging fire turned into embers. Their conversation was filled with laughter, and it wasn't long until Daniel fell asleep in the chair he was sitting in. Keith picked him up and placed him in bed, and he remained there until morning.

The following five days were filled with the same antics and every evening Daniel enjoyed fishing with Wade. They went to the same area every day, and by the last day, Daniel had grown accustomed to fish flapping around the bottom of the boat. He even learned how to clean and prepare the fish and was encouraged to do so with Wade's custom knife.

Wade continued to tell stories he learned as a child, hoping that Daniel would benefit from their lessons. Daniel, in return, began to open up and offered his thoughts about his parents, Olivia, school, and Josh.

On the day they were preparing to leave, Wade surprised Daniel with a gift. He handed Daniel a red book. Daniel flipped it open; the pages were empty. "What's this?" he asked.

"It's a journal. Years ago, when I was going through some difficult times, I wrote in a journal to help me understand my own thoughts. I know sometimes that talking about your feelings is difficult but writing in a journal is easy. You can ask any questions and be able to internally search for the answer. No one will judge you and you might be surprised just how therapeutic writing can be."

"Thanks," Daniel said.

Everyone shared a heartfelt embrace before Keith and Daniel left, and they promised to see each other again soon. Keith repeatedly honked the horn as they drove away, and Daniel energetically waved. He played with the journal the entire drive home, rubbing his thumb across the pages. When they arrived, Daniel ran inside to tell his mother about all his adventures.

Keith, stiff from the long drive, took his time and started unloading the car. He dropped the load of bags in the hallway and was met by Marilyn with a kiss on the cheek, Daniel at her heels babbling on about fishing. Keith started to cough and excused himself to go outside and continue unpacking the car. However, loaded down with luggage, Keith clutched his chest and collapsed on the porch.

He regained consciousness in the hospital; Marilyn was pacing, and Daniel was sitting slumped in a chair at the end of the bed.

"What happened?" Keith asked.

Marilyn grabbed his hand and started crying. She whimpered, "You just collapsed on the porch. I thought you were dead."

Their conversation caught the attention of the doctor. He entered the room and said, "I'm glad to see you awake. We're not yet sure what happened, and we'd like to keep you in the hospital overnight for observation."

"Okay," Keith responded, his voice weak.

The doctor turned to Marilyn. "He's in good hands. Go home and get some rest."

Their current situation was a drastic and sudden change for everyone, especially Daniel. He did his best to weather the emotional storm, but just as he was coming to terms with reality, Marilyn said, "We're going home. Your father is staying in the hospital overnight."

It was a tense drive home. Daniel did not say anything because he did not want to upset his mother. The entire way she repeated, "I need a drink." Once they arrived, Daniel remembered the story Wade told him about the flower and the bee. Wanting to show how much he cared, Daniel approached his mother in the kitchen as she was pouring herself a drink. He snuck up behind her and gave her a hug. Marilyn threw up her hands and said, "What the heck are you doing, Daniel? I don't need a hug right now; I need a drink! Go to your room and start unpacking. Throw your dirty stuff in the laundry."

Deflated and angry, Daniel grabbed his belongings and locked himself in his room. He sat on the end of his bed and noticed the journal Wade gave him. He opened it to the first page and began writing:

*Yesterday, I was fishing, swimming, canoeing, and having the time of my life. Now my dad is in the hospital and my mom has started drinking and yelling at me again. I wish I could go back to Uncle Ross and Wade's place. I could fish every day and canoe around the lake with Wade. But I would miss my dad. I hope my dad comes home tomorrow. I hate it here when it's just me and Mom. I hate it when she yells at me and I hate her for the way she makes me feel. Why is this happening to me?*

# CHAPTER SIX

## Like Mother, Like Son

The news that Keith's cancer had returned did not take long to circulate amongst the neighbourhood. Soon after, he, Marilyn, and Daniel were receiving well wishes and thoughts of sympathy from family and friends. Keith continued his chemotherapy and did his best to face the onslaught of pain and discomfort with the same quality of determination and positivity he amassed after his first experience with cancer. However, as the weeks wore on, both Keith and those around to him noticed a slow decay in his physical appearance. He began losing weight and before long he looked like a walking skeleton. Completely hairless, he would stumble around the corridors of the hospital as he endlessly clung to hope that his situation would improve. As time wore on, his conditioned worsened, and Keith finally realized that he would not get better. A decision was made that, for the sake of his family, he would live his remaining days in the comfort of his home.

Marilyn, experiencing an ambush of emotions over the previous months, did her best to be a comforting presence to her dying husband. But she relied on alcohol more and more as the days passed. To make it worse, her doctor prescribed her several medications, including Xanax. She was advised not to mix her medications with alcohol, but her dependence on alcohol made it impossible not to. Instead of being attentive and at Keith's side, Marilyn could be found lying on the couch, her glazed eyes circumnavigating the room as her numb mind enjoyed relief from anxiety. She barely had the strength to do anything, and most of the responsibilities she had were forced upon Daniel.

Every day, Daniel would wake up early and make a fresh pot of coffee for his mother. The aroma was usually enough to rouse her out of bed. By the time she placed herself at the table, Daniel had prepared breakfast—usually toast with jam and a glass of milk. He would pack his own lunch and before leaving for school, Daniel would give his sedated father a hug and kiss.

While at school, Daniel found comfort in forgetting about what was happening at home. His friends were a sanctuary, but their ability to provide relief was nothing compared to when he was around Olivia. They would spend hours together after school and took turns walking each other home. Olivia would listen to Daniel as he read his journal entries to her. She was compassionate and supportive. Her capability to empathize with Daniel gave him the strength of positivity and the courage of wisdom. So often, after such moments of vulnerability, they could be found holding each other. Olivia would rub Daniel's back until he felt better, and in return, he would hold her hand in his and gently brush her knuckles with his thumb. They loved each other but were too young and naive to understand exactly what they were experiencing. There were many attempts to discuss their feelings for each other, but their nerves always got the better of them.

On many occasions throughout the week, Daniel was a welcome guest at the Roubles' dinner table. William and Natalie were aware of what was happening due to the frankness of Daniel's stories. They would often send him home with leftovers for Marilyn.

On this day, as he arrived home with a backpack full of spaghetti and garlic bread, Daniel noticed a familiar car in the driveway. He realized it belonged to Dr. Fitzgerald. Daniel ran inside and was surprised to see the doctor, Marilyn, and Keith sitting at the dining room table.

"Well, hello there, young man. It's good to see you," Dr. Fitzgerald said as he smiled. He gave Daniel a hug. He was carrying a small piece of paper in his hand and placed it in his pocket. "I just came over to check on your parents. How are you doing, Daniel?"

"Good."

"And what about school?"

"Good."

"Since I'm here, is there anything you'd like to talk about?"

"No."

"A man of few words." Dr. Fitzgerald chuckled. "All right then, Daniel. I'm here if you need to talk."

"Okay."

"It was good to see you," Keith said, barely able to stand. His body shook with the effort.

"You too. Remember to rest."

"All he does is rest," Marilyn said as she escorted Dr. Fitzgerald to the door. She extended her hand and said, "My prescriptions please."

"Oh . . . silly me. I almost forgot," the doctor said, reaching into his pocket. He produced the small piece of paper and gave it to Marilyn. She crumpled it in her hand.

Daniel watched as Dr. Fitzgerald drove away. Before his car was beyond sight, Marilyn said, "I'm going to the pharmacy, Daniel. Look after your father until I get back."

She was already out the door by the time Daniel was able to respond. He went to the kitchen and found his father sitting at the table. He unloaded his backpack and scooped a portion of spaghetti into a bowl. He warmed it up, along with a slice of garlic bread, and gave it to Keith.

"Thanks, son. I hope you know how much I appreciate this. You've done a lot around here and I am grateful."

Daniel looked at his decaying father and said, "I know."

They continued to talk until Keith finished his dinner. Not once did they mention, nor want to consider, the inevitable. Afterwards, Daniel took his father by the arm and helped him up the stairs and into bed. He covered him with a blanket, and they shared a hug. Not having the strength to converse further, Keith said, "Good night, Daniel. I'll see you in the morning."

Nearly an hour later, Daniel heard his mother return home. He could hear as she searched the kitchen for a clean glass, all the while whispering, "That lazy kid" and "He never puts anything back where it belongs."

Several minutes later, Daniel heard his mother's footsteps coming up the stairs. She opened his door and demanded that he join her in the kitchen. When he arrived, Marilyn was standing in the corner, pointing to a collection of dishes in the sink. "What did I tell you?" she asked, her eyes red and a vein protruding from her forehead. "What did I tell you, Daniel! Clean up after yourself. Do you have any idea what I do around here?"

Daniel looked around the main floor and noticed that every room was a mess. "Doesn't look like you do anything around here."

"Don't you start with me," Marilyn exclaimed as she opened the bottle of Xanax and removed the cork from a bottle of wine. She placed a pill in her mouth and took a swig from the bottle. "You have no idea what I go through. I'm here all day long while you get to go to school and play with your friends."

"What would you like me to do? Quit school?"

"No, you idiot. But I need you to help out around here more often."

"Whatever, Mom," Daniel said as he tried to leave, but Marilyn grabbed his arm. She dragged him in front of the bathroom mirror and said, "You know what I see?"

"A drunk," Daniel responded. Without warning, Marilyn slapped him across the face.

"No! I see a disrespectful excuse for a son who doesn't do anything to help his mother."

"Leave me alone!" Daniel yelled. He was strong enough now to push Marilyn out of the way. She fell backwards against the shoe rack. Enraged, she grabbed Daniel by the neck and pushed him onto the front porch.

"Guess who's sleeping on the porch tonight?" Marilyn exclaimed as she threw Daniel's jacket on the ground. Shocked, Daniel stood still and watched as his mother closed and locked the front door. He pounded on it for several minutes but there was no response. He started to cry and began cursing his mother's name. He sat on the step nearest to the ground and placed his head between his knees.

Mr. Johnston, who was applying a layer of wax to his car, overheard the commotion because his garage door was open. He had grown accustomed to Marilyn's nightly outbursts but decided not to get involved. However, upon hearing Daniel crying, Mr. Johnston reluctantly approached and sat next to him.

"Hello, Mr. Johnston," Daniel said as he wiped his tears with his sleeve.

Mr. Johnston took a deep breath and said, "It's tough listening to your mother every night, but I don't envy what she has been going through. Nor do I envy what you've gone through, Daniel."

"What do you mean?"

Mr. Johnston paused and wrapped his arm around Daniel's shoulder. "It must be difficult watching your father get closer to death with every passing day. I'm positive it has been stressful for your mother."

"I don't care about my mother anymore. She's mean to me all the time."

"Well, someone has to care about her. If not her son, then who?" Mr. Johnston asked, but there was no response from Daniel. "I'm sure your mother is scared, and I can imagine how anxious she is about the future."

"Anxious?"

"Scared, Daniel. Your mother is scared and I'm sorry that she's taking it out on you. Come on, I want to show you something," Mr. Johnston said as he escorted Daniel into his garage. "Everything I care about, and have cared about, is in this garage. This was my wife," he said, pointing to a portrait on the wall. "She also died of cancer not too long ago. So, I can understand what your family is going through. I'm still dealing with the fact that she's gone and sometimes it hurts to look at her picture."

"What's that one?" Daniel asked, pointing to a picture of a group of men standing in front of a ship that had HMCS Skeena painted on the bow.

"That is the ship I served on during the war. We escorted convoys across the Atlantic and rescued survivors from U-boat attacks. Most of those people in the picture are gone," Mr. Johnston said as his voice trembled. His eyes shone with tears. "There's only eight surviving crew members, including myself. After the war, I dealt with many different emotions and, like your mother, I took them out on those closest to me."

"You did? What happened?" Daniel said as he continued looking around the garage.

"I had some dark thoughts, Daniel, and I wouldn't be here if it wasn't for the love and support of my wife. I wasn't myself and she knew there wasn't much she could do to help except be there when I needed her."

"But my mom hates me. She made me sleep on the porch."

"She's not herself, Daniel. I know it's difficult but try not to take it personally. I think your father was expecting this to happen because several weeks ago he asked me to look after you if something happened."

"He did?" Daniel said with wide eyes. He turned to look at Mr. Johnston.

"Yes. So, instead of sleeping on the porch, how about you come inside and sleep in the spare room?"

"Really?"

The invitation was a welcome surprise for Daniel. With a smile, he gladly accepted Mr. Johnston's offer. They continued to talk as Mr. Johnston finished waxing his car, and it was the first time in a while that Daniel opened up about how he was feeling to someone other than Olivia. He expressed his fear about losing his father to cancer and his anger toward his mother for the way she treated him. He mentioned his lack of focus in school and how he felt about Olivia.

Mr. Johnston smiled and said, "This Olivia reminds me of my wife. Anyone could talk to her about anything, and she would listen. She was a great listener and no matter what the topic was, she always had an answer—some type of response that would help. She was wise, and everyone appreciated her. That's why I loved her so much—for her compassion and her ability to understand and help others. But most of all me."

"That's how I feel about Olivia."

Mr. Johnston stopped what he was doing and said, "Do you love her?"

"How do you know if you love someone?"

"Well, being in love is like happiness. You think about that person constantly and want to spend time with them. They make you happy and you want to make them happy."

"Then, yes, I think I love Olivia," Daniel said as he looked at his reflection in the surface of the car.

"Then don't hesitate to tell her because she might just love you back."

Daniel helped remove the wax and by the time they were finished, both he and Mr. Johnston were tired enough to entertain the thought of going to bed. They closed the garage and went inside his house. The interior was immaculate, and everything was neatly put away. Daniel watched as Mr. Johnston hung his set of keys on a nail next to the door frame.

"Maybe you can help my mom clean our house?" Daniel asked.

Mr. Johnston laughed as he showed Daniel to the spare room. They walked down a hallway, past a bedroom where Daniel noticed a picture of Mr. Johnston's wife placed on a pillow next to where he slept. "You can use this bathroom here, and you can sleep here," he said.

"Thank you, Mr. Johnston."

"Don't mention it. Anyways, I promised your father I'd help. Now, get a good night's sleep and we'll have a chat with your mother in the morning."

The following morning, Marilyn awoke to the sound of someone knocking on the door. Groggily, she looked around and wondered why Daniel had not made coffee. Her frustration turned to shock when she opened the door to notice several strangers holding cleaning equipment. They introduced themselves and advised Marilyn that an anonymous friend had paid for the cleaning service. Marilyn was bewildered but she welcomed the strangers into her home and watched, with pleasure, as they cleaned, scrubbed, and sorted the chaotic mess throughout the house.

It was nearly two hours later when their work was complete. "You guys are amazing! I can see my floor again," Marilyn said. "Please, I must know who—" She was interrupted by another knock at the door. It was Daniel accompanied by Mr. Johnston. "Where have you been, Daniel?" she yelled as those who witnessed the sudden change in demeanour took a step back.

"You made me sleep on the porch, remember?" Daniel said as tensions rose.

"I did no such thing!"

"Yes, you did!" Daniel cried; the cleaning crew decided to slip past Marilyn as he spoke. Once outside, they took a deep breath and looked at each other with raised eyebrows.

"Not to worry, Marilyn. I took care of him last night and fed him breakfast this morning. He slept in my spare room," Mr. Johnston said. Marilyn closed the door without offering any gratitude for his actions.

She was about to continue her verbal assault on Daniel when she noticed Mr. Johnston handing the cleaning crew some money. She smiled and instead of chastising Daniel for raising his voice in front of strangers, Marilyn enjoyed a cup of coffee accompanied by a shot of whiskey. "Thank god it's the weekend," she said as she sat on the living room couch. She looked around and enjoyed the fact that she would not have to lift a finger for the remainder of the day.

Her moment of relaxation was interrupted by a sound upstairs.

"Help! Help!" Keith cried.

Daniel and Marilyn ran up the stairs and found Keith on the floor. He was stuck in between the toilet and the bathtub; feces covered his backside and was smeared on the side of the toilet seat where he slipped off.

"Ah . . . I can't do this anymore!" Marilyn shouted. "I'm calling 911. You're going back to the hospital."

Daniel was left alone with his father as Marilyn went to the kitchen to call an ambulance. He covered his nose and breathed through his mouth. Keith was too weak to move. Daniel tried to help, but the smell made him gag. He suffered through the urge to vomit and, as the sound of sirens approached, Daniel did what he could to provide his father with some decency. He cleaned up the fecal matter that had dried on the toilet. He was about to clean his father when Keith delicately grabbed Daniel's wrist and said, "You don't have to do this, son."

Moments later, two medics arrived and assisted Keith onto a stretcher. Daniel waited in the kitchen and watched as he was loaded into the ambulance; members of the community gathered around the house.

"This started off being a great day and now this," Marilyn grumbled as she laced her shoes. "Stay here, Daniel. Clean the mess in the bathroom," she demanded.

Daniel, not wanting to give his mother another excuse to make him sleep on the porch, did as requested. As he scrubbed the floor and tried not to puke, Daniel noticed splattered blood on the side of the bathtub. He lay on the floor and started coughing, imagining the blood leaving his father's mouth and pretending to wipe his cheek with his sleeve. Daniel remained on the floor, the smell of bleach on his fingers.

There was a sudden rush of emotion throughout his body followed by a sensation of pain, and he drew his knees up to his chest. He cried so hard that his muscles started to burn. There was pain in his chest and his lungs could not retain enough oxygen. Daniel cried until he felt exhausted. Too tired to move, he remained on the bathroom floor and waited until he felt strong enough to get up.

He wiped his tears, washed his hands, and looked at himself in the mirror. He stared into his bloodshot eyes and breathed heavily. "You know what I see?" he said to himself. "I see a baby. I see a wimp. I see a—" He was interrupted by a knock at the door.

It was Olivia.

"I'm so sorry, Daniel," she said when he opened the door. She wrapped him in a hug as he began to cry again. "I just heard what happened and came over as soon as I could. Are you okay? Is there anything I can do?"

Daniel, trying to make sense of what he was experiencing, said, "I just want to be left alone."

"Please, Daniel, the last thing you should do is to be is alone. I can stay with you, and we can—"

"We can what, Olivia?" exclaimed Daniel. His tone surprised her, and she took a step back. She had never heard him raise his voice. "Pretend that everything is hunky-dory? Pretend that I'm happy and that my father isn't going to die and that my mom doesn't hate me?"

"Oh, Daniel, I'm sure your mom doesn't hate you."

"What would you know about it. You and your perfect family. Your perfect parents."

Olivia, with as much contempt as Daniel, said, "You should be grateful for how my parents have included you, fed you, supported you, and treated you as their own son."

"Gimme a break."

"They love you, Daniel, and they have only wanted to make your life easier. Can't you see—"

"What?"

"That I love you, too," Olivia said, tears welling up in her eyes. "And that I care about you."

Daniel, too angry to understand what was being expressed, said, "That's the last thing I need. Now please, Olivia, I just want to be left alone." He closed the door in her face.

Olivia walked home and cried the entire way.

Daniel was unable to rid himself of the anger and resentment festering within him. He noticed the bottle of whiskey Marilyn used to top up her coffee. Without hesitation, Daniel removed the cap and began drinking straight from the bottle. He started to shake as the alcohol burned down his throat. He coughed and suddenly regretted his decision when he realized that his mother would know some of her alcohol was missing.

He frantically looked around the kitchen and realized he could replace what he drank with water. He placed the bottle under the tap and, with precision, substituted the amount he consumed. He put the bottle back on the counter where he found it and, as the numbing effects of the whiskey flowed through his veins, he stumbled up the stairs and lay on his bed.

There he remained as he enjoyed a reprieve from the present—his mind empty and his fingertips tingling. He covered himself with his blanket as his room spun around him.

# CHAPTER SEVEN

## Unlucky Thirteen

Daniel awoke on the day of his thirteenth birthday to the sound of the phone ringing and his mother's voice straining to seem lucid to whomever she was talking to. He heard her crying, then she yelled, "Daniel, wake up! We have to go to the hospital."

It had been two months since his father was admitted to the hospital. Since then, there had been a steady decline in his health. As the days passed, the hope that Keith would recover began to disintegrate just as his body did.

For Daniel, a trip to the hospital was not out of the ordinary. However, as they got closer, he suspected something was wrong because Marilyn did not stop crying. They were greeted by Dr. Fitzgerald at the main entrance, and they followed him, in silence, to an area of the hospital they had grown accustomed to seeing. The staff, usually upbeat and welcoming, were instead sombre and kept to themselves as Daniel and Marilyn walked past. Daniel recognized his father's room because it had a picture of Keith on the door. The picture was from a time when Keith's health was not an issue. He had tanned skin, a big smile with gleaming teeth, and a head full of hair. It was a stark contrast to the skinny, pale body that lay on the bed in the room.

The walls of Keith's room were filled with cards and pictures from family and friends. On both sides of the bed were bouquets of flowers hiding the assortment of machines keeping him alive. Usually, upon recognizing his family, Keith would open his eyes and greet them; this time, there was no movement at all.

"Please, sit down," Dr. Fitzgerald said. He took a deep breath before continuing, "We all knew this day would come. It has been my goal to prepare you for the decision that needs to be made. Unfortunate as it is, I'm sorry, Marilyn and Daniel, that it befalls you. Last night it was decided, by me and several colleagues, to transfer Keith to palliative care and suggest turning off his life support. This is why I asked you to be here. Marilyn, as Keith's spouse, and Daniel, as his son . . . I would like your permission to turn off his life support. We will provide enough morphine to keep him comfortable and allow him to pass without pain or discomfort."

Marilyn began to cry again. Daniel looked at his father and then at Dr. Fitzgerald. "Dad is going to die?"

"Yes," the doctor said, his hand on Daniel's shoulder. Marilyn's sobbing intensified.

"Is there nothing else you can do?"

"His body is failing, Daniel. He's beginning to lose function in certain areas and there's nothing we can do to stop it from happening."

"If we turn off his life support, how long will it take before he . . ."

"It could be hours . . . maybe a day."

Daniel wiped his tears away with his sleeve and said, "Okay."

Dr. Fitzgerald looked to Marilyn. She was barely able to keep her head up, and all she could do was nod.

Shortly after, a nurse came into the room and assisted Dr. Fitzgerald in the removal of Keith's life support. Keith was lying on his back, and Daniel watched as his breathing slowed. Silence surrounded them as both Daniel and Marilyn were tortured by internal thoughts of death and what life would be like without Keith. An hour later, after what seemed like an eternity, Daniel watched as his father took his last breath.

Daniel cried until his stomach ached. He looked at his father's body and watched as the fleshy tone of his skin turned to the colour of ash.

Suddenly, Marilyn embraced her son as her tears flowed into his hair. She wrapped her arms around his shoulders and pulled him in close. Daniel was comforted by the warmth of her body, but it did not last long because Dr. Fitzgerald entered the room. He spoke softly. "My deepest sympathies to you both. I'm sure you have questions about what to do next. Here is some information for you to take home," he said, handing Marilyn an envelope.

"Where are they taking dad?" Daniel asked as two nurses covered Keith with a sheet and started manoeuvring his bed.

"They're taking him to the hospital mortuary."

"And then what will happen to him?"

"Then he will be transferred to the Lakeside funeral home in Port Dalhousie."

Dr. Fitzgerald patiently answered all of Daniel's questions. Marilyn remained silent, but her cravings for a drink were making her antsy. Noticing the change, Dr. Fitzgerald delicately said, "Keith has left instructions in the envelope. I know it's difficult but try to go through them later today."

Marilyn quickly got up and, without thanking Dr. Fitzgerald or the hospital staff, walked toward the exit. "Hurry up, Daniel," she said without looking back. Even though he had numerous questions, Daniel chose the lesser of two evils and followed his mother outside and into the car.

She closed her door, started shaking, and said, "I don't know if I can drive home." She snapped her fingers and began rummaging through her purse until she produced a pack of cigarettes. As she lit one, Daniel was quickly engulfed in smoke and began to cough.

"Isn't that how dad got cancer?" Daniel asked.

"Don't start!"

"I'm only pointing out the obvious, Mom."

"Daniel! I swear to God, I'll leave you in the parking lot if you keep this up," Marilyn exclaimed as Daniel rolled down his window.

Marilyn finished her cigarette and felt relaxed enough to attempt the drive home. However, as soon as the nicotine in her system demanded to be replaced, she quickly lit another cigarette. She went through four cigarettes before they got home.

Marilyn quickly exited the car and left Daniel alone. He watched as she hurriedly unlocked the front door. Daniel remained in the car by himself for some time until he gathered the strength to confront his mother about her habits. He placed his hand on the seat and felt something crumple. He looked down to notice the envelope Dr. Fitzgerald had given them. Daniel opened it and read, "Last Will and Testament of Keith Theodore Harris. It is my wish that the executor of my estate will by my brother, Ross Harris . . ."

There was a knock on the window, and Daniel jumped. He sat up straight and gasped, but he relaxed when he saw it was his neighbour. He rolled down the window and said, "Hi, Mr. Johnston."

"Hi, Daniel," Mr. Johnston replied, noticing the smell of smoke emanating from the car. "I just came over to see how you were doing. Did you visit your father this morning?"

Daniel lowered his head, wiped a tear from his eye, and said, "He died this morning."

"Oh, Daniel," Mr. Johnston said, his voice trembling. "I'm so sorry to hear that. Your father was a great friend and neighbour. His service to the community will be remembered by many."

"Thank you."

"Where's your mother? I hope she's doing okay?"

"She's inside, getting drunk."

"Oh. Uh . . . what's that you have there?" Mr. Johnston pointed to the envelope on Daniel's lap. Daniel handed it to him. "Oh, I see. Would you like to come inside? I can make you a sandwich."

At that question, Daniel realized how hungry he was. "That sounds good to me. Do you have any pop?"

"I don't have Coke, but I do have Pepsi."

"That'll do."

Upon Mr. Johnston's suggestion, Daniel brought the envelope with him, and as he enjoyed his lunch, Mr. Johnston read the documents inside. After some time, he said, "I'm not sure if your mom is sober enough to handle this. Would you like me to contact your Uncle Ross? It looks like your father has made him the executor of his will."

"What's an executor?"

"Ah . . . caretaker."

"Sure, you can call him."

As Daniel continued his lunch, he could hear Mr. Johnston talking on the phone with his uncle. His neighbour returned before he took his last bite of his sandwich. "Your Uncle Ross said he received the same documents nearly a week ago. Looks like you father was well prepared."

"Prepared? How does someone prepare to be dead?"

"Well, if you have assets or money set aside, its best to detail a plan for who and where you want your possessions to go. When my wife died, she left money for our grandchildren's education, and the remainder, including this house, she left to me. When I die, I'll give everything to my son."

"Did my dad leave anything for me?"

"I did notice an envelope with your name on it . . . Here it is!" Mr. Johnston said as he gave it to Daniel.

"That's my dad's handwriting," Daniel said as he opened the envelope.

"Perhaps, you might want to wait until you're alone to read that. Sometimes, when reading something personal so near to death, it can be overwhelming. I wouldn't want you to make this day any worse than it already is, son. Leave it for another day."

Daniel did as was suggested. He accepted a chocolate chip cookie that Mr. Johnston had baked that morning. He dipped it in milk and once finished, he thanked him for lunch. He was about to leave when Mr. Johnston stopped Daniel at the door and said, "I forgot to mention that your Uncle Ross said he will be driving down tomorrow. He plans on going through your father's will and he wants to help prepare for the funeral."

"Funeral?" Daniel said nervously as he was confronted by painful memories. He had the strength to say goodbye to Mr. Johnston, but his tears came to the surface again and by the time he arrived home, Daniel thought he was going to be sick.

Consumed with grief, Daniel searched his home, calling out his mother's name, but there was no response. He eventually found her passed out on the living room couch. She was wearing Keith's leather jacket. There was a half-empty bottle of whiskey on the coffee table and next to it was a small bottle containing some pills. Not wanting to aggravate her, Daniel sought solitude in his room, but he couldn't sit in the silence with his emotions.

Like his mother, he thought that consuming alcohol would help relieve him of such burdens. He made his way into the living room, noticed that his mother had not moved, and without hesitation, Daniel took three large gulps of whiskey. He felt the burning sensation in his throat and started to cough. He quickly covered his mouth and placed the bottle back onto the coffee table. Marilyn adjusted herself and drunkenly scoured the room with one eye, but Daniel had already made it back to his room.

Ten minutes later, he was succumbing to the effects of the alcohol. Oblivious to the fact that his father had died only an hour prior, Daniel remained motionless, passed out on his bed until morning.

The following day, the sound of Marilyn stomping up the stairs startled Daniel. He sat up in his bed and cringed as the pain in his head radiated from ear to ear. Seconds later, Marilyn burst into his room, grabbed him by the hair, and hoisted Daniel out of bed. "Ow . . . Mom, stop! What are you doing?" he yelled.

"You think you can steal from me?" Marilyn said as she forced Daniel in front of the mirror that hung on the back of his bedroom door.

"What are you talking about?"

"My whiskey! You drank from it, didn't you?"

"What? No!"

"Don't you lie to me, young man. You're not supposed to be drinking at thirteen years old."

"You're not the best example, Mom."

"Oh, shut up," Marilyn yelled as she slapped Daniel across the back of the head. "You know what I see, Daniel? I see a thief. I see a liar. I see a—"

Marilyn was about to continue the onslaught of demeaning remarks when she noticed a familiar car pull into their driveway. "No. What is he doing here? He better not have brought that red-skinned, treaty check–wastin', fetal-alcohol, no-good Indian onto *my* property."

Daniel turned around, looked out his bedroom window, and noticed Uncle Ross and Wade exiting their car.

"Goddamnit!" Marilyn exclaimed as she ran down the stairs; Daniel followed. She opened the door as they were about to climb the stairs leading to the porch and said, "He's not welcome here, Ross. You know better."

"Marilyn," Ross said softly. Wade was behind him with raised hands in front of him. "The last thing we want to do is cause you more pain. Please . . . we're here to help."

"You can help by leaving!" Marilyn exclaimed as she clenched her fists and straightened her arms by her sides.

"We're not going to do that. We're family and we want to be here to grieve together. It's what Keith would have wanted," Ross said as he slowly climbed the stairs and approached Marilyn.

"What would you know about it?"

"He made me executor of his will, Marilyn. I need to be here to get everything in order."

"Well, you're not welcome to do it here," Marilyn said as Daniel moved past her.

"Hi, Daniel," Wade said with a smile.

"Don't you dare talk to my son. He told me about your fishing trips and the motor that magically stopped working. You probably molested Daniel and threatened him, didn't you?"

"That's enough, Marilyn!" Ross exclaimed. "We've all been through a lot the past twenty-four hours. Perhaps—"

"I lost my husband!"

"And I lost a brother! Daniel lost a father!"

"Okay, everyone," Wade said. "Let's let cooler heads prevail. Maybe I can take Daniel to McDonald's while you and Ross discuss the details."

After several more exchanges, including reassurances from Daniel that he was comfortable going with Wade, Marilyn whispered in his ear, "Fine. You can go with Wade, but don't listen to what he says, Daniel. He's a pathological liar."

Daniel shook his head, his eyebrows furrowed. He ignored her comment, and he and Wade made their way to McDonald's.

Wade, normally the conversationalist, remained silent as they drove. He watched Daniel and noticed that he was massaging his forehead and had difficulty keeping his eyes open. They arrived, and after discussing what to order, Daniel found an empty table. Shortly after, Wade placed a tray between them and began dispersing the food. Daniel devoured his lunch, inhaling his quarter-pounder with cheese and quickly moving onto his fries, dipping them into the small containers of ketchup.

"You must have been hungry," Wade said, noticing Daniel was finished and he was only a few bites into his burger.

"Starving."

"Doesn't you mom cook for you?"

Daniel looked at Wade with a raised eyebrow and said, "Gimme a break. My mom hasn't cooked in months."

"You look healthy."

"Thanks to the Roubles and Mr. Johnston."

"Yes, the Roubles—I've heard of their generosity. It's Olivia, right?"

"What about Olivia?"

"I thought she was your girlfriend."

"Nah, she's just a friend."

"So, you still don't have any feelings for her?"

Daniel took a moment to think about Wade's question and said, "Haven't thought about it lately."

"Well, what do you think about?"

"My dad," he said, trying to hold back tears.

"I'm so sorry, Daniel. He was a wonderful man and a great father to you. He served his community, lived passionately, and did his best to remain grateful for every moment. You father lived a fulfilling life."

"Yeah, but not a long one," Daniel whimpered.

"It's not the length of life that determines how someone lived, but the quality of life. Your father may not have lived a long life, but it was filled with happiness, compassion, and love."

Daniel reached for some napkins, placed them against his face, and started crying. Wade sat next to him and placed his arm around his shoulders. Several minutes later, once Daniel was feeling better, Wade took his place across from Daniel and said, "Have I ever told you the story about Margaret the salmon? It's a story my dad used to tell."

"It's not like that bee and the flower story, is it? A lot of help that did."

"No, it's a different one. Would you like to hear it?"

Daniel nodded as he sipped his pop.

"Well, one day, after enjoying many delightful years in the open ocean, Margaret the salmon woke up and noticed something was different."

"I didn't know that salmon slept," Daniel interrupted.

"Well, they do in this story. Anyways, she woke up and felt that something had changed. She wasn't sure what it was, but she followed her intuition and swam all the way across the ocean. Along the way, Margaret the salmon was met by hundreds of other fish that looked like her and they were all headed in the same direction.

"One morning, she noticed that the bottom of the sea was getting closer and soon after, she was at the mouth of a small river. She could sense the difference between the salt and fresh water and, wanting to continue her journey, started swimming upstream but stopped when a small pebble said, 'Aren't you afraid to die?'

"Margaret the salmon looked at the pebble and said, 'What do you mean? I'm not going to die.'

"The pebble laughed. 'Of course, you are. No fish ever makes it out alive. This river is a one-way trip, didn't you know?'

"Margaret the salmon was confused, and she remained where she was and watched as hundreds of her fellow fish swam past her. 'Are we going up this river to die?' she asked the nearest fish.

"He responded, 'Yeah, but what a ride it's going to be.' Immediately, Margaret the salmon stopped swimming and she floated back into the ocean. She remained there alone and feared what would happen. However, her instinct was too strong to defy, and she reluctantly began swimming up the river.

"Along the way, she swam into some old friends, jumped over boulders, avoided predators, and felt the rush of the river flow around her. She continued to swim, and as the water began to calm, Margaret the salmon watched as lifeless fish floated past her. 'What's happening?' she asked, frantically looking around her and noticing that her belly was beginning to swell.

"'Mother nature is what's happening. Just relax and be happy that you've arrived,' the nearest fish to her said. Margaret the salmon watched as the fish happily expelled hundreds of eggs along the bottom of the river. Several minutes later, her lifeless body floated downstream. Scared of what would happen to herself, Margaret the salmon resisted the urge to push.

"'Just let go,' a group of rocks beneath her said. 'We've been here for a hundred years and watched thousands of fish like you come and go.'

"'But I'm scared,' Margaret the salmon said.

"The group of rocks looked at each other and said, 'You have no choice.' Margaret the salmon continued to resist but her efforts were in vain. Moments later, she expelled all the eggs from within her, and as they collected in the crevasses between the rocks, she felt the need to rest, and she closed he eyes for the last time."

"Wait, so you're saying that Margaret the salmon didn't know she was going to die?" Daniel asked.

"No, she resisted the fact that she was going to die, and it nearly stopped her from fulfilling her purpose. Death is inevitable and the earlier you accept the fact that you're going to die, the earlier you'll live without fear, restraint, or regret. Your father experienced this after his initial diagnosis of cancer. Did you not notice a stark difference in your father after he finished chemotherapy?"

"Yes, he seemed happier and when he went back to work, he never worked overtime. We spent more time together and he smiled a lot more. He would take my mother out on dinner dates, and he bought me gifts even though it wasn't my birthday or Christmas."

"That's exactly what I'm talking about, Daniel. Like Margaret the salmon, who was afraid to die and fulfill her purpose in life, your father accepted the inevitable and it allowed him to live a more meaningful, happier life. Yes, we should be sad that your father died but also be happy that he lived a fulfilling life."

By the time Wade completed his story, both he and Daniel had finished their lunch. As they drove home, Daniel pondered Wade's story. Wade did his best to answer all of Daniel's questions about life and death. By the time they arrived home, Daniel was feeling better, and he had a superficial understanding of why his father died.

However, soon after Wade and Uncle Ross left, the pain accompanying the loss of his father increased as he passed family photographs hanging on the hallway walls. He found his mother slumped on the couch; the coffee table was covered with envelopes and folded paper. A large glass filled with alcohol and ice sat on top, its condensation soaked up by the documents. Marilyn grabbed the glass, drank the contents, and slurred, "The funeral is next Saturday."

# CHAPTER EIGHT

## A Moment of Bliss

The day of the funeral had arrived. Daniel was sitting on the stairs waiting for Marilyn as she rummaged through her purse, looking for her Xanax prescription. She took one and washed it down with a mouthful of vodka. She covered her mouth with a closed fist and stared at the floor, then collected herself and started wiping debris off her black skirt. Daniel watched as she groomed herself, his mind consumed with disgust, until he heard a car pull into the driveway. He stood when Wade got out of the passenger side and greeted him and Uncle Ross. They shared a heartfelt hug but stopped when Marilyn made her presence known. "Enough of that, you three. The last thing I need right now is for my son to become a homosexual. Let's get this over with," she said as she walked past them. She got into the car, rolled down the window, and yelled, "Daniel, did you remember to bring your speech?"

Daniel searched his pockets and realized that he had left his speech on the kitchen table. Not wanting to give his mother a reason to get frustrated, he went inside the house and found the envelope where he left it. He picked it up but hesitated when he noticed his mother's bottle of Xanax on the counter. Without contemplating her reaction, Daniel opened the bottle, took one pill, and placed it inside his jacket pocket. He put the bottle back where he found it and ran down the hall and outside.

He sat next to Wade in the back seat of the car, not realizing that he forgot to grab his speech. He and the others in the car watched the neighbourhood pass as silent contemplation consumed them.

They passed by a procession of police officers when they arrived at the funeral home. They were greeted by friends and extended members of their family. Daniel did not recognize half the people there. After cordially accepting their condolences, he, Marilyn, Wade, and Uncle Ross entered the funeral home.

The main area was filled with conversation, bouquets of flowers adorning every empty space along with pictures of Keith throughout his life. Daniel made his way into the parlour and, beyond a room full of chairs, saw the casket containing his father's body. There was a small line of people waiting to pay their respects; Daniel patiently stood in turn. He hesitated to look inside when it was his turn. However, his courage resumed when he felt Wade's reassuring hands clasping his shoulders. "We'll do it together," he said, offering a slight smile.

They approached the casket and when Daniel looked upon his father's body, he was surprised by what he saw. There was no recognizable feature of his father. There was a separation between this body and Daniel's memory. There was no smile, no warmth in Keith's skin. Any sense of life had disappeared and, as the seconds passed, Daniel became more uncomfortable. He started to quiver, and Wade suggested they find a place to sit down. Wade then excused himself to find Marilyn and Uncle Ross. Several minutes passed and Daniel closed his eyes as he tried to forget about what he just witnessed. He wanted to leave but he felt someone sit next to him and clasp his hands.

"Olivia?" Daniel said, surprised. He hugged her and as her warmth and the recognizable smell of her hair comforted him, Daniel cried into her shoulder and said, "I'm so happy to see you."

"I'm happy to see you too, Daniel," she said, patting his back.

"I've missed you."

"I've missed you, too."

"I'm sorry I haven't been around or returned your calls lately."

"It's okay, Daniel. You've been through a lot," Olivia said as Daniel lifted his head from her shoulder. He looked into her amber eyes and was lost in their beauty. She handed him a napkin and he wiped the tears from his face. "You've been through a lot, and I want you to know that I'll always be here for you when you need someone to talk to."

"Thanks, Olivia, but I don't feel like talking right now. Actually, I feel like I'm going to be sick," Daniel said as he covered his mouth with his hand. He manoeuvred past Olivia, through the crowd of mourners, and into the bathroom. He found an empty stall and hovered over the toilet bowl for a while. Several minutes passed and nothing happened. Beginning to feel better, Daniel splashed his face with water from the sink. As he dried himself off, he caught his reflection in the mirror.

He looked at himself with contempt and disgust, his mother's voice calling him a *liar* and *worthless* in his mind. He punched the mirror, causing it to shatter. The shock of it made Daniel instantly regret what he had done. He looked around to see if anyone else saw what happened, but he was alone. Breathing a sigh of relief, Daniel buttoned his suit jacket and felt the pill he had placed within the pocket. He removed it and, without hesitation, swallowed the pill. He wiped the excess water from his mouth, exited the bathroom, and resumed his position next to Olivia.

She took his hand, noticing he was nervously rubbing his knuckles, and did not let go as the pastor introduced himself. As the first guest was being welcomed to speak, Daniel was experiencing a sense of calm so intense that he had difficulty keeping his eyes open. He lethargically looked around the room and thought he was in a dream. The sound of crying and the crinkling of tissues was prevalent as he fell deeper into himself. However, his serenity was interrupted when he thought he saw his father's body move. He jumped and the movement shocked Olivia. Concerned, she escorted him into the foyer and asked, "What's wrong with you, Daniel?"

"I took a pill I stole from my mom." He giggled. "This is the greatest feeling ever."

"You did what?"

"Relax, Olivia, I think I need to sit down."

"You can't go back in there. Not like this," Olivia said as she escorted Daniel outside.

"Whoa, that's better," Daniel said as he sat down on the wooden banister. "The air smells so fresh. Actually, it smells funny. What is that, anyway?"

"Just stay here, Daniel. I'm going to get my dad."

"Okey dokey."

Daniel began rocking side to side and made a clicking noise with his mouth, imitating a pendulum. He took another deep breath and noticed the same awkward smell coming from the far side of the building. Fascinated, he followed the scent until he could hear people talking and laughing, and as he approached, Daniel recognized a familiar face and said, "Josh! Josh Thompson!"

"Holy cow! Dan the Man Harris, is that you? What the heck are you doin' here?" Josh said as he raised his hand for a high-five. "You remember Tom and Gary Goodwin."

"Sup," Tom said.

"How's your head?" Gary laughed. Tom and Josh joined in.

"That's right, bro, the last time we saw you was when you did a header into the old canal," Tom said as he inhaled what looked to Daniel like a cigarette. He watched as Tom held his breath and exhaled thick smoke.

"Yeah, we left you for dead. Good thing Peanut Butter Pete was there," Gary said as Tom passed him the awkward-looking cigarette. Daniel watched as he inhaled and held his breath but ended up coughing, to which Tom and Josh laughed.

"Weak," Josh said.

"Novice," Tom added. "Yeah, I totally forgot about Peanut Butter Pete saving your ass. That was crazy."

"So, what brings you here, Dan?" Josh asked as he inhaled.

"It's my dad's funeral today."

"Oh crap, man. I heard about your dad. I'm so sorry, man," Josh said.

"Me, too, Dan. Life sucks, man," Tom said.

"Yeah, life sucks," Gary added.

"Hey, how about a toke to make things better?" Josh said, handing Daniel the weird-looking cigarette.

"What's this?" Daniel asked as Josh, Tom, and Gary laughed.

"It's weed, man. You live under a rock or somethin'?" Josh said as he showed Daniel what to do. Daniel inhaled and wanted to cough but Josh covered his mouth and said, "Nope, don't be a wuss. Hold it in for three . . . two . . . one! Yeah, Dan is the man. Okay, now exhale."

"Atta boy!" Tom said.

"Way to go," Gary added.

"How do you feel?" Josh asked.

Daniel hesitated as a host of strange, yet enjoyable sensations surged throughout his body. He felt a tingling in his fingers and experienced an insatiable need to eat. He smiled at Josh and said, "I feel great."

"Well, do it again!" Josh exclaimed as Daniel inhaled a second time. The enjoyable effects became more prevalent as he continued. He broke down into a fit of laughter as Josh, Tom, and Gary joined in. It took several minutes until, out of energy, they could not laugh any more.

"Daniel?" asked Olivia, her voice emanating from the entrance to the funeral home.

"Daniel!" Josh, Tom, and Gary mocked in unison as they broke down in laughter again.

"I better get going, guys," Daniel said, wiping the tears from his bloodshot eyes.

"Definitely," Josh said.

"Drop by the house sometime. We'll have to do this again," Daniel said as he left the group. He stumbled his way to the entrance of the funeral home and placed his hand on the brick exterior to prop himself up. He giggled the entire way as the mixture of marijuana and Xanax flowed through his body. Daniel found Olivia, who was looking for him with haste in her eyes when she said, "You smell funny. Why are your eyes red?"

Daniel giggled in response.

"Everyone is looking for you. Your mom is doing that flare thing with her nostrils that she does when she gets angry," Olivia continued as she took Daniel by the arm and escorted him into the chapel. "The pastor said you prepared something to say."

Everyone breathed a sigh of relief as Olivia escorted Daniel toward the podium. Marilyn's obvious irritation was amplified by a protruding vein in the middle of her forehead. Daniel was not sober enough to notice the eyes staring at him in judgment. He grabbed the podium with both hands and did his best to remain upright. He reached within his jacket pocket and noticed it was empty. In a moment of anxious sobriety, Daniel remembered that he placed his speech on the kitchen counter before hastily stealing one of his mother's pills. He looked upon the silent crowd before studying the grain in the wooden podium.

He started to giggle and could not stop, so he covered his mouth with his hand as tears of laughter streamed down his face. Everyone watching him was confused, but most assumed he was suffering from an abundance of emotion. Olivia was the first to rise, followed by Uncle Ross. They comforted Daniel by rubbing his back before escorting him out of the chapel and into the foyer. Uncle Ross informed the pastor to continue as Olivia remained with Daniel.

Daniel's laughter subsided and as his moment of bliss was over and the saddest day he ever experienced resumed, the only thing that consumed his mind was how to achieve the euphoric level of happiness he had just experienced.

The funeral had finished by the time Daniel came to the sobering conclusion that he was in for some kind of discipline. However, Marilyn remained cordial as everyone flooded the foyer to offer sentiments and converse over happier memories of the deceased.

An hour later, with Olivia still by his side, Daniel realized it was time to leave. He stumbled trying to enter the car and nearly fell asleep as they followed the hearse to the cemetery; nothing was said along the way.

Everyone gathered around an open pit and watched as Keith's coffin was delicately lowered into the ground. Marilyn and Daniel stood next to the gravestone. Daniel's actions at the eulogy caused an internal boiling of anger and frustration for Marilyn, and she would have unleashed a torrent of degrading comments toward Daniel if they had been alone. Underneath her black shroud, Marilyn clenched her fists as her jawbone flexed. She experienced a surge of anxiety and started to sweat. Ross noticed when she started shaking and began to cry. Her sister, Roxy, tried to comfort her but her consoling efforts were in vain. Marilyn's knees weakened; her father stood on her other side as he and Roxy held her upright.

Daniel was oblivious to his surroundings and his mother's torment as he watched his father's casket come to a stop. In his hallucinogenic state, Daniel imagined he was a worm, and his body was crushed when the casket lay upon him. This thought shocked him out of his stupor as he felt a soft, delicate hand grab his. "It's time to go," Olivia said. Daniel watched as flowers and handfuls of dirt were strewn upon the casket before some final offerings of compassion were given. Soon after, Uncle Ross and Wade drove Daniel and Marilyn home. After sharing a heartfelt hug with Daniel, Uncle Ross said, "We'll be back tomorrow to finish up a few things."

Marilyn and Daniel waved, but as soon as Wade and Ross were out of sight, she took him by the collar and dragged him into the house. She made Daniel stand in front of the mirror and said, "What do you see?"

"Not now, Mom!"

"Yes, now!" Marilyn said as she slapped the back of his head.

"What did you do that for?" Daniel said, coming face-to-face with Marilyn, his brow furrowed.

"Because you're an ungrateful moron and an idiot. Now, tell me what you see!"

"I'm not doing this today," Daniel said, trying to leave the bathroom, but Marilyn did not budge.

"Okay, you want to know what *I* see?"

"Not really," Daniel scoffed.

Marilyn grabbed Daniel by the hair and yelled, "I see a loser of a son who had this one chance to say goodbye to his father, but instead decided to get high and laugh like an idiot in front of everyone we know. You're a scumbag son who disrespects his father on the day of his funeral by acting like a moron instead of showing any regard for the dead. After everything he did for you—"

Daniel pushed her away from him. She bumped the back of her head against the banister. Marilyn, with fists clenched, raised her hand, and slapped his cheek. Daniel stood in defiance and looked into her eyes. She turned her hand around and, with her exposed diamond ring, slapped Daniel a second time. The force of the blow and the sharpness of the diamond resulted in a four-inch laceration in his cheek. Blood dripped down his face and collected on the floor. Immediately regretful, Marilyn grabbed a towel from the bathroom and gave it to Daniel. It stopped the bleeding, but it was quickly losing its ability to absorb liquid.

They got in the car and drove to the hospital where he was hastily tended to. After Marilyn provided a falsified reason for the cut, Daniel's cheek was stitched and covered with a thick bandage. Marilyn searched for remorseful words during the drive home, but by the time they arrived, her need to cure her woes overcame her need to apologize. She went directly into the kitchen, mixed herself a drink, and topped it off with a Xanax.

Twenty minutes later, Daniel found her asleep on the couch. He clenched his jaw, and the pressure caused him to wince in pain. He gingerly touched the bandage with his index finger and noticed dried blood underneath his fingernails. He washed them and noticed more dried blood on his shirt collar. He went upstairs and sat on the edge of his bed. Physically and mentally exhausted, he slumped over, placed his hands over his head, and grabbed his journal that was underneath his bed. He began writing.

*Forty stitches! I cannot believe that just happened. I should have told the doctor that my cunt of a mother slapped me. Maybe I could have charged her with assault. The cops would have arrested her, and she'd spend the night in jail. Maybe I could ask for a restraining order. That way she wouldn't be able to come close to me. Maybe I'd get to move in with Uncle Ross and Wade and never have to see her drunk ass again. She needs to understand that she can't treat me like this anymore. I know what I need to do. I need to stand up for myself now that Dad's gone. No one else is going to do it for me. And I don't care if she finds out that I stole her booze or her pills. If she can drink and take pills, then I can drink and take pills. If she can get high, then I can get high. I can't wait to meet up with Josh again. I don't care if Mom thinks he's a bad influence—she's worse! And now that Dad's not around and Mom spends her days passed out on the couch, I can do whatever I want. I don't give a crap what she thinks and if she ever hits me again, I'm going straight to the cops.*

# CHAPTER NINE

# The Cardinal

The day after the funeral came quickly enough. Marilyn, who had remained asleep on the couch throughout the night, was awoken by a knock at the door. The piercing morning light inhibited her ability to focus as she placed her unbalanced feet one foot in front of the other. She opened the door and, with the smell of alcohol on her breath, said, "You can come in, but not him."

"Is Daniel here?" Uncle Ross asked. "I have a few things to discuss with him, too."

"I have no idea where he is. You woke me up. Did you at least bring Timmies with you?"

"Medium double-double, right?"

"Oh, you are a Godsend."

Ross looked around the house and noticed the buildup of dishes in the sink, month-old dust on surfaces, cobwebs stuck to the ceiling, and a pile of dirty clothes that had been thrown down the basement stairs. The smell of rotten food came from the fridge and, as unpleasant as it was, Ross remained cordial and said, "Would you like some help tidying the place?"

"No, the maid service comes will be coming in a few days. They'll take care of it."

"Maid service?"

"Yeah, our neighbour Mr. Johnston takes care of it for us. Said he promised Keith to look after us."

"That's very generous of him. I should introduce myself."

"He lives next door. He's usually in his garage looking after his car," Marilyn said as she enjoyed her coffee; the caffeine provided her with enough focus to continue.

As Ross placed several envelopes on the table and began dispersing the contents, Wade, who was patiently waiting on the porch, heard Daniel's voice, and followed it into Mr. Johnston's garage.

"Hey, guys," Wade said. He caught them both by surprise because they were underneath the car. "Sorry to bother you, Daniel, but your Uncle Ross wanted to speak to you."

"Hi, Wade," Daniel said energetically.

"Time to give Fanny an oil change," Mr. Johnston grunted as he manoeuvred into a standing position.

"Your car's name is Fanny?" Wade laughed.

"Yep, Fanny the Falcon. Hey Daniel! Remember to replace the bolt after all the oil has drained."

"Okay," Daniel said as the clicking sound of a ratchet could be heard. "Done!"

"Great. Now, come on outta there and clean up. From what Wade tells me, it looks like your Uncle Ross needs to speak with you."

Daniel was hesitant because he knew the bandage on his face would result in queries. It did. Wade questioned what happened, and Daniel lied and said, "I fell off my bike while trying to do a stunt."

"Yeah?"

"Well, I fell over my handlebars and cut my cheek. Got forty stitches."

Wade's concerns were soon rendered mute as Daniel reassured him that he was okay. He washed his hands and, as requested, joined his mother and Uncle Ross in the kitchen. Once again, his explanation, taken at face value, was enough to quell Ross's concerns and provide Marilyn with a reason to add some Baileys to her coffee.

"Wade and I will be going back up to Algonquin today," Ross said as he placed most of the paperwork into an envelope. He handed it to Marilyn and said, "Put that in a spot where you'll remember it." She excused herself to the living room couch as he and Daniel continued their conversation. "I know this might be confusing, but within these documents is your father's last wishes." Ross handed Daniel a small envelope and said, "This contains a registered education savings plan your father started for you. As you can see, it has nearly twelve thousand dollars in it—"

"Twelve thousand dollars!" Daniel said, his eyebrows raised.

"Yes, but it has to go to toward your post-secondary education."

"What's post-secondary?"

"College or university."

"Oh, okay. But what happens if I don't go to college or university?"

"Then the money will go to your mother."

"Screw that!" Daniel exclaimed loudly, hoping Marilyn would hear him.

Ross looked at Daniel with a raised eyebrow and said, "And your father left you an additional two thousand dollars to spend as you wish."

"Two thousand," Daniel said as his jaw opened. "I can spend it on anything I want?"

"Yes."

"Awesome!"

Daniel's response irritated Ross. He clenched his jaw and, regaining his composure, asked, "Would you rather have a father or the money?"

Daniel reclined in his seat and remained quiet. "He also left you this letter," Ross continued. Daniel, with hands shaking, accepted the small envelope and opened it. He removed several pieces of paper and noticed his father's handwriting, but the emotion associated with it prompted him to quickly put it away. "Perhaps, when you're ready," Ross said as he placed the remaining paperwork into a large brown envelope and gave it to Daniel. "Before we go, I wanted to let you know that you're always welcome to stay with me and Wade."

"I can?" Daniel asked. He sat up straight and looked into Ross's eyes.

"Yes, whenever you want. Just call and we'll come down and get you, or you can take the bus. Or maybe you'll be driving by then . . . whatever."

"Thanks."

"You're welcome. Promise me that you'll look after yourself. It seems to me like your mother might also need some help."

"Gimme a break." Daniel laughed. "The only help she needs she finds in the bottom of a bottle."

"That's what I'm talking about, Daniel. Your mother isn't dealing with Keith's death in a healthy way. I understand the need to dull emotions, but the path your mom is taking will only lead to more problems. Please promise me that you'll try to look after your mother."

"Why? She doesn't look after me. She doesn't cook anymore, doesn't clean the house, doesn't talk anymore. I can't even remember the last time she gave me a hug."

"Well, I can give you a hug," Ross said as he embraced Daniel. His warmth gave Daniel a sense of security and Daniel wished it could remain; however, it was not long after when they were exchanging farewells. Reluctantly, Daniel promised his Uncle Ross that he would do his best to look after his mother. He watched as Ross and Wade drove away while wondering when he would see them again.

Marilyn went back inside and poured herself another drink as Daniel caressed the corners of a check worth two thousand dollars. "Going to the bank, mom!" he exclaimed without pausing for a response.

He jumped on his bike and started pedalling as fast as he could. Sweating and out of breath, Daniel arrived at the bank and approached the teller. "I have a check I would like cash."

"All of it?" she asked, peering over her glasses that were hanging off the end of her nose. "I'm sorry, young man, but you're only permitted to withdraw a maximum of fifty dollars per transaction. What do you want with two thousand dollars anyway?"

"I just want it for some nunya."

"Nunya . . . what's nunya?"

"Nunya business."

"Look, young man, I don't appreciate your tone and if you want to access your money, then you'll have to follow the bank's policy."

"Okay, sorry," Daniel responded. "Well, I'll just take the fifty dollars then, but can I have some quarters, too?"

Daniel watched with wide eyes as the teller counted his money. He placed it in his pockets and, before leaving, asked, "When can I take out more money?"

"You're permitted to remove a maximum of fifty dollars per day."

"Thank you," Daniel exclaimed as he exited the bank and went directly to the hobby shop across the street. He eagerly perused the isles, looking for the newest model of the F-14A Tomcat. He grabbed the box, which was nearly as big as he was, and after paying for it, Daniel was happily surprised by the amount of money remaining. He biked two blocks to the comic bookstore and purchased the most recent Amazing Spider-Man along with ten packs of Upper Deck hockey trading cards. With all his cash spent and only change in his pockets, Daniel walked to the nearest arcade and spent the next two hours immersed in the electronic worlds of Contra, Ms. Pac-Man, Donkey Kong, and Missile Command.

The following weekend, Daniel surprised Olivia when he showed up unannounced at her house. William was raking leaves and noticed

Daniel approaching. He removed a pair of gloves, and they embraced each other as if they were father and son.

"It's good to see you, Daniel," William said.

"It's good to see you too."

"How are you doing? How's your mother?"

"Oh, we're doing okay. It's tough not having dad around," Daniel said as he looked to the ground.

"I can only imagine. Natalie was thinking about dropping by to see you mom. Do you think she'd like that?"

"I don't know. She can try. I mean, my mom hasn't done much the last week. She wakes up only to sleep on the couch all day," Daniel said, nervously scratching his stitches.

"That's a nasty cut on your cheek."

"Yeah, it happened when I fell off my bike," Daniel said. Ashamed that he lied and wanting to see Olivia, he asked, "Is Olivia here?"

"She sure is. She'll be happy to see you."

"Really?"

"Yeah, I think she's in the kitchen doing homework. She's been moping around the house since the funeral," William said as he escorted Daniel inside. He opened the front door and said, "Look who I found!"

"Daniel!" Olivia screamed as she jumped from her chair and ran down the hall. When they collided, she nearly knocked Daniel over. She started jumping in place and said, "I'm so happy to see you. What happened to your face?"

"I'll tell you about it later."

"Hi, Daniel," Natalie said from the kitchen. "I'm making chocolate chip cookies. Would you like one?"

"Sure!"

Everyone gathered around the kitchen table and enjoyed fresh cookies and milk. The chocolate chips were melting, and everyone thoroughly enjoyed the cookies. The delightful silence was interrupted when Olivia asked, "Why did you come over?"

"I was wondering if you'd like to see a movie with me."

"Really? Today? What movie?" Olivia asked excitedly.

"*Home Alone* was just—"

"Oh, Daddy, can I go see *Home Alone* with Daniel, please?" Olivia asked, looking at her father with puppy-dog eyes.

"Yes, as soon as you're done homework."

"I just finished! Ask Mom," Olivia said, to which Natalie nodded in the affirmative.

"Okay, I'll drive you to the theatre."

"Yes!" Daniel and Olivia exclaimed together.

Thirty minutes later, they arrived at the Pen Centre. William said goodbye and watched with a smile on his face as they walked hand in hand until they were out of sight. At the theatre, Daniel paid for Olivia's ticket and bought snacks and pop. They laughed every time their hands touched when reaching for popcorn. When the lights dimmed, Daniel was overcome with happiness.

After the movie finished, they walked through the mall, laughing, talking, and imitating scenes from *Home Alone*. Daniel spent the rest of his money on ice cream, and he bought Olivia a New Kids on the Block sweater. She swung the bag like a pendulum while they waited for William to pick them up. It was not long until Daniel was dropped off at his home. Olivia walked him to the door and gave him a hug and a kiss on the cheek and said, "Thanks for today, Daniel. It was really good to see you, and I had lots of fun. I hope we can get together again soon."

"Me too," Daniel said before watching them drive away. He took a deep breath before entering his home but, as expected, he found his mother asleep on the couch.

A few days later, Daniel was sweeping the porch when an old, rusty Chevrolet Chevette parked on the street in front of his house. It used to be white and was currently eroding away from the rust collecting on its frame. The doors creaked open and out from the driver's seat stepped Tom Goodwin followed by his brother Gary, and Josh Thompson.

"What are you guys doin' here?" Daniel asked.

"You told us to drop by sometime, remember? Or were you too messed up from the ganga?" Josh asked as Tom and Gary laughed.

"Ganga?"

"Reefer . . . spliff . . . grass."

Daniel squinted at them.

"Weed, you idiot. Remember, at your dad's funeral?"

"Oh, yeah. You got any more?" Daniel asked.

"Nah, I stole that from my parents," Josh said.

"We don't have any cash, anyways," Tom said.

"Yeah, no cash," Gary added as he wiped his nose with his wrist.

"I have money," Daniel.

Josh, Tom, and Gary shared a harmonic, "You do?"

"How much do you have?" Josh asked.

"About fifteen hundred dollars."

"Fifteen hundred dollars! Where did you get that much money from?"

"I got it after my dad died."

Josh, Tom, and Gary began jumping up and down. They approached Daniel and slapped him on the back. Josh asked, "Do you have any idea how much weed you can get for fifteen hundred bucks?"

"No, how much?"

"You could fill your living room."

"Well, what are we waiting for?" Tom said. "Let's go see the Cardinal."

"Yeah, the Cardinal!" Gary added.

"Who's the Cardinal?" Daniel said.

"Get in the car and we'll tell you on the way," Josh said.

Daniel followed his companions without hesitation. Ignoring consideration for his responsibilities at home, and not seeing it as worthwhile to advise his mother as to his whereabouts, he found his spot behind the driver's seat and soon they were off. They made jokes at each other's expense and started playing air guitar and drums when "Thunderstruck" by ACDC came on the radio. The antics continued after a quick stop to withdraw some money. Daniel asked, "Where are we going anyway?"

"Niagara Falls," Josh said as he punched Daniel in the shoulder and laughed.

The beat-up car trudged along the highway, remnants of burned oil emanating from the tail pipe as blue smoke. They arrived at a large property with a derelict-looking house. The roof was partially covered in a black tarp and the once off-white paint was peeling, the fallen pieces collecting on the ground where they fell. The surrounding yard was filled with weeds and crab-apple grass and there was a broken sidewalk leading up to wooden stairs covered in exposed nails. Josh knocked three times and soon after, the front door opened.

A man who looked almost too big for the doorframe greeted them with a smile and invited them inside. Daniel was the last to enter and he watched as the large man hobbled on his left leg and grunted as he settled into a well-used spot on the creased leather couch. The interior of the house wasn't any nicer than the exterior; it smelled like beer and feces. There was a large television on the other side of the room. Josh, Tom, and Gary made themselves comfortable as Daniel stood nervously next to the door.

"Get over here!" the large man snarled. "Take this spot next to me."

Daniel feared him and as he walked past, he noticed underneath the man's short black hair was a long scar that began above his right ear and went around the circumference of his skull. He also noticed that the man had skin the same colour as Wade's. After Daniel sat down, the large man asked, "And who are you?"

"I'm Daniel . . ." he said, swallowing thickly under the glare of the man's bloodshot eyes.

"All right, Daniel, and you know these guys?"

"Ye-yes."

"No need to be scared, little man. What are you doin' hangin' around these fools?"

"He's the money!" Josh said.

"Oh, really? Well, you're welcome here anytime. My name is Tony."

"They called you the Cardinal," Daniel said, pointing to his friends.

"My last name is Cardinal. I don't care what you call me if you got cash, little man. Show me what'chu got."

Daniel reached into his pocket and produced a twenty-dollar bill.

"Okay, this guy means business here!" Tony laughed. Everyone but Daniel joined in. "Wait here," he said before hobbling his way upstairs. A few tense minutes later, he sat back next to Daniel and threw a plastic bag in his lap filled with marijuana. "That's what twenty bucks gets ya."

"Well, don't just stare at it!" Tom said.

"Bust it open!" Josh said as he took the bag from Daniel. He watched as Josh carefully rolled a portion of it into a shape like a cigarette. He lit the end, inhaled, passed it to Daniel, and said, "Time to man up."

Daniel imitated Josh and, shortly after holding his breath, began coughing. Everyone else started laughing and soon, Daniel joined in. He was about to take another puff when Tony took it from him and said, "Sharing is caring, little man." He started singing, "Pass the dutchie 'pon the left-hand side," to which Josh, Tom, and Gary joined in.

They remained in Tony's house well into the evening, their boisterous laughter sporadically interrupted by a knock at the door. Tony had business to conduct. They had smoked most of the marijuana by the time Daniel suggested they leave. Tony gave each of them a hug. He grabbed Daniel by the shoulders and said, "I like you, little man. You're always welcome here. As long as you have cash!"

"Thanks, Tony."

There was a collective goodbye as they got back into the dilapidated Chevette. On the way home, Josh suggested they get McDonald's. Daniel offered to pay with the remainder of the fifty dollars. They sat around a table and hastily consumed their dinner.

"Boy, did we ever get lucky today at Tony's," Josh said.

"Yeah, he was in a pretty good mood today," Tom said.

"He must have taken his meds," Gary said.

"What do you guys mean?" Daniel asked.

"Flip of a coin with that guy," Josh commented as he wiped his mouth with his sleeve. "Sometimes he's in a good mood, and other times you just want to get the heck outta there."

"Yeah, once I saw Tony pull a knife on a guy for laughing at a joke that he thought wasn't funny," Tom said.

"And do you remember the time he sat on Squidge and nearly suffocated him because he was sitting in Tony's spot?" Gary added.

"Who is Squidge?" Daniel asked.

"Don't worry about it," Josh said. "And you know when it's gonna happen, too. He gets those crazy eyes, and he looks at ya like he's gonna kill ya."

Josh, Tom, and Gary continued to share infamous stories about Tony. Daniel did his best to listen but the drugs in his system made him incredibly hungry, and after scarfing down his meal, all he wanted to do was sleep.

"Rookie!" Josh exclaimed before suggesting to Tom that they take Daniel home. Before leaving, Daniel purchased a meal for his mother in a moment of sympathy. He regretted not advising Marilyn about his whereabouts and thought McDonald's might lessen the reaction he expected from her.

It was impossible to be inconspicuous because the sound made by the Chevette's exhaust bounced off every possible surface. Josh stuck his head out the window and said, "What are you doing next weekend?"

"Going with you guys back to Tony's?"

"Atta boy!" Josh exclaimed to Tom's and Gary's delight.

Tom revved the engine and initiated a pathetic attempt to squeal the tires. All that resulted was the sound of the engine backfiring. Daniel watched as the car barely made it up the hill; he waited until he could no longer see the one working headlight.

He took a deep breath and entered the house. He cringed as he opened the door but, to his surprise, Marilyn was not on the other end. He searched the house and found her passed out on the couch, a glass with melting ice on the coffee table next to an empty prescription bottle. He looked upon her with disgust, but the words of his Uncle Ross came into his mind: *Please, look after your mother.* Daniel placed a blanket on his mother and turned off the lights.

Not wanting to waste the extra meal, Daniel took it to his bedroom and ate it all. Still stoned, and content with a full belly, he stared at the ceiling. Unable to move, he started to giggle and imagined himself doing everything all over the next weekend.

# CHAPTER TEN

# Descent

The weekend could not come quickly enough. The thought of getting high again consumed Daniel and as the week progressed it seemed as if life, absent of this temporary, superficial happiness, was proving too much to handle. At school, he could not focus because all he could think about was his need to get high. While sitting at his desk, Daniel would watch the minutes pass and daydream about the antics in Tony Cardinal's living room.

In preparation for the weekend, each day after school, Daniel went directly to the bank and withdrew the maximum daily limit of fifty dollars. By the time Saturday arrived, he had amassed a sum of three hundred dollars. As he sat on his porch, he counted the bills repeatedly before placing them in his pocket. As he waited for his friends to arrive, Daniel tapped the bulge as if concerned it would not be there when needed. Daniel began bouncing on his toes as the sound of Tom's Chevette rounded the corner. The amplified noise came from a section of the muffler secured by a wire coat hanger. Josh leaned out the window, playfully taunting Daniel to join them. Before leaving, Daniel opened the front door just enough to stick his head through and tell Marilyn that he was going out with his friends. There was no response.

His increasingly absentee mother was barely coherent enough to render a response to Daniel's announcement. She spent her days in a continuous downward spiral and her lack of motivation to improve resulted in another mixture of alcohol and Xanax. She lumbered around the house, stumbling over piles of laundry and garbage. The kitchen counter was covered with dirty dishes and in the near-empty pantry was a loaf of mouldy bread, a jar of peanut butter, and half a dozen boxes of Kraft Dinner. The only time Marilyn felt the need to portray sobriety was on Tuesday afternoons when the weekly cleaning service would drop by and clean the house.

Marilyn would forget what day it was, and she would often wake up in the middle of the night and reach over to feel if Keith were there. Sometimes, upon noticing an empty spot, she would walk throughout the house, calling his name. Often, at night, Daniel would find her in the hallway looking at old family photographs, tracing the pictures with her fingers. He would scoff to himself and say in an unsympathetic tone, "Dad's dead, Mom, remember? Go back to sleep."

She was beginning to have difficulty with the simplest tasks like cutting an apple or folding sheets. And she constantly had to prop herself up while walking due to an increasing sensation of vertigo.

Daniel was ignorant of such drastic changes in his mother because he was consumed by his own pursuits—mainly getting high with his friends. Marilyn turned on the television and relaxed on the couch, swishing an ice-cold mixture of vodka and sprite. She held on to the remote and stared at the floor, trying to remember something Daniel told her.

As Marilyn was misplacing what Daniel had said, he, Josh, Tom, and Gary had arrived at Tony Cardinal's house. They were surprised when their usual parking spot was taken, as well as every other available space on Tony's property and the street. Dusk was approaching and as they skipped up to the house, they could see that it was filled with people. They sauntered up to the door and noticed the sound of music and boisterous conversation. Energized by their resolve and curiosity, they entered the house and joined the party. They squeezed through the throngs of strangers as the smell of sweat and spilled alcohol emanated from the dilapidated carpet. They made their way into the living room and found Tony sitting in his spot on the couch. Upon recognizing Daniel, Tony bounded from his seat and gave Daniel a hug that squeezed the air out of his lungs.

"It's great to see you guys!" Tony said. His voice was barely louder than the music. "You got cash?" he said, rubbing his thumb in a circular motion against his fingers.

"Daniel does," Josh said.

"Of course, he does. Follow me!"

Tony took them upstairs and into what Daniel assumed to be his bedroom. There was a sheet covering the window and a mattress on the floor, its boundary covered with dirt. On the other side of the room was a decaying couch. Next to it was a large safe. Tony knelt next to the safe, started spinning the dial, and said, "Sit down, guys, be with you in a minute. How much money you got, little man?"

Daniel reached into his pocket and produced the full sum contained within. Josh, Tom, and Gary gasped, and it got Tony's attention. "How much is there?" he asked.

"Three hundred," Daniel said proudly.

"Holy crap!" Josh exclaimed and Tom and Gary high-fived each other.

"Man of the hour," Tony said as he produced a large plastic bag of marijuana. He tossed it into Daniel's lap, his eyes wide with joy. "What's the first rule again?"

"Sharing is caring!" everyone said unanimously.

Daniel proudly removed some marijuana from the bag and gave it to Tony. He watched as Tony placed it into a coffee bean grinder and diced it into a fine, dust-like texture. Then, with focused determination, he delicately rolled it with a small piece of paper, and after licking the ends, gave it to Daniel and said, "You do the honours, little man."

Daniel ignited the end and inhaled deeply. After several seconds, he exhaled while coughing and passed it to the left.

"Little man is learning fast," Tony said. "With that much money, you ever think of selling it?"

"No, don't be silly." Daniel laughed.

"I'm serious, little man. You and your boys could make a mint!"

Josh, Tom, and Gary perked up and noticed Tony's raised eyebrow. "You really think so?" Josh asked.

"Oh yeah. You can hit up Clifton Hill and sell it to all the tourists."

"No way!" Tom said.

"Yeah, no way!" Gary added.

"How much could we make?" Josh asked.

"Sky is the limit. You buy it from me for twenty dollars a bag and sell it for forty on the street. You can double your money in just a few hours."

"But we don't have any money."

"Little man over here has bank. How much you got?" Tony said, his red eyes staring at Daniel.

"Twelve hundred bucks," Daniel said proudly.

"Holy crap," Tom said. "We could make a killing!"

"Yeah, a killing!" Gary added.

"What do you think, little man?" Tony asked while rolling another joint. "You want to do business with me?"

Hesitant, Daniel looked at his friends as they stared back at him with encouraging eyes. They were unanimously nodding their heads as the room filled with smoke. Daniel was about to respond when Tony said, "I want to show you something."

They followed Tony down the stairs that led to the basement. There was a large black door with several locks on it. Tony opened each one and, before revealing what was inside, he said, "I don't let everyone down here. So, whatever you see, keep it to yourself. If word gets out, I'll know it was one of you and I'll tear your nut sack off. Got it?"

After receiving a terrified yet unified agreement from the four friends, Tony opened the door. From within the room came light so bright that they had to shield their eyes. They followed him inside and, once their eyes adjusted, they could see the entire basement was filled with marijuana plants so tall that they reached the ceiling. Daniel, Josh, Tom, and Gary looked upon the spectacle with awe as their mouths dropped to the floor. They noticed several fans pushing the air around and the smell emanating from the plants was potent. Tony walked toward the nearest plant and exposed one of its branches. "Isn't it beautiful," he said as their eyes adjusted. "Only two more weeks until they're ready."

"How long did it take you to grow all these?" Josh asked.

"About four months."

"How much is all this worth?" Tom asked.

"Should get at least thirty thousand out of it."

There was a unanimous gasp from everyone. Tony turned around, looked at Daniel, and said, "So, you want in?"

Daniel, not contemplating the possibility of any negative situations, said, "Hell yes!"

"Atta boy, little man!" Tony said as Josh, Tom, and Gary shared in his excitement. "In two weeks, you guys can help me harvest this crop and then we'll have a hell of a time sellin' and smokin' it. But that's enough business for now. Let's head upstairs and join the party."

Tony, after locking the door, led the four rambunctious friends into the living room where they laughed, smoked, drank, and danced until they were exhausted.

Several hours later, as the crowd began to disperse, Daniel found himself propped against a speaker, trying not to fall asleep. He tried to remain awake and noticed Tony talking to someone and pointing in his direction. The man he was talking to was skinny and had a scruffy face. He wore baggy clothing and a Toronto Blue Jays baseball cap. He was carrying a bottle of Coca Cola as he and Tony approached. "This is the kid I was talkin' about," Tony said as he grabbed Daniel by the neck and shook him lightly. "Little man, I want you to meet Squidge."

Daniel, barely able to keep his eyes open, extended his limp hand. He looked into Squidge's eyes and was surprised by how small his pupils were. "Squidge?" he slurred. "Why is your name Squidge?

"Actually, my name is Shawn—"

"Because you can do this!" Tony yelled as he picked him up by the waist. He threw Squidge onto the couch and sat on him. The pressure caused Squidge to slip in between the cushions, his exposed right arm providing proof that he was stuck in the crevasse. Tony laughed as Squidge painstakingly manoeuvred himself free.

"You in the mood for a little pick-me-up?" Squidge said as he straightened his shirt. Daniel was surprised by how fast he talked. "Come on over here, little man, I've got something special for ya."

Squidge took Daniel by the shoulder and escorted him into the kitchen. He opened a small bag containing cocaine and dumped the contents onto the counter. Daniel watched as he used a credit card to divide it into three separate lines. When he finished, Squidge looked at Daniel and said, "My boy Tony says you have money."

"Yeah . . ."

"Well, you got any cash on ya?"

Daniel reached into his pocket and produced a twenty-dollar bill. Squidge took it from him and tightly rolled it into a cylinder. Daniel watched as he placed one end into his nostril as the other end hovered over a section of cocaine. He inhaled it in one quick motion and said to Daniel, "Your turn, little man. Now, don't hesitate! Just stick it in there and suck it all back as fast as you can."

Daniel did as was instructed, and as the cocaine entered his system, he felt a surge of energy and a distinct taste dripping down his throat.

"Atta boy!" Squidge said as he and Tony slapped Daniel on the back in jubilation. "Cardinal, your turn."

Daniel watched as Tony snorted the remaining cocaine but did not notice when he placed the twenty-dollar bill into his back pocket. He tilted his head up toward the ceiling and started shaking. His eyes opened wide, and he let out a loud yell. "Hell ya! Who's ready to party?"

Daniel, enjoying his newfound energy, returned to the living room, and started jumping in place. He felt as if he could touch the ceiling with his head and his actions caught the attention of his friends. Josh approached first and asked, "What the heck are you doing? Ten minutes ago, you were about to pass out and now you're bouncing off the walls."

"I did cocaine!" Daniel said with jubilation.

"What? Where? Who?" Tom asked to which Daniel pointed in Squidge's direction.

"Squidge is here!" Josh said.

"Yeah, can we get some?" Gary asked.

"I dunno, let's go ask," Daniel said.

Daniel took Josh, Tom, and Gary to where Squidge was. After a short conversation, as well as confirmation that Daniel would pay for the cocaine, they followed Squidge into the kitchen and took turns doing lines. Moments later, they were all yelling and screaming at each other. In their energetic state, they went outside and chased each other before being motivated to smoke another joint coupled with beer and pizza.

The party continued for the next two days. It was not until dawn approached on Monday morning that Daniel realized he should be getting ready for school.

He woke up lying on a couch in the backyard. It was next to a fire pit and he recognized the potent smell of smoke on his clothing. He brushed a layer of ash off his arm as he painstakingly adjusted himself into a seated position. His mouth was dry, and he craved water but the nearest thing to him was a half-drunk bottle of beer, so he drank that instead. He spat out the beer and puked after ingesting a discarded cigarette butt. He wiped his face, looked around the yard, and noticed that he was alone. Daniel stood up and had difficulty balancing, but he eventually found his way into the house. It stank of beer, smoke, sweat, and rotting food. There were people passed out on the floor and the only sign of life was that they were breathing. He found Tony asleep on the couch, but he did not want to wake him.

So, Daniel waited on the front steps. Tom's Chevette was no longer there. He tried to conclude how to get home, but he was unable to form a cohesive thought.

He was about to start walking when he heard someone approach. He looked up with half-closed eyes and recognized Squidge. "You need a ride home, little man?" Squidge asked.

"Yes, please."

"Come on then."

Daniel followed Squidge to his car and was surprised when he opened the door to a brand-new 1990 black-on-black Mustang GT with gold rims.

"This is yours?" Daniel asked with astonishment.

"Yep. It's all mine. Got it at a great price, too," Squidge said as he started the V8 engine. The rumbling of the exhaust gave Daniel goose bumps.

"How much did it cost?" Daniel said as he secured the seat belt.

"I got it for ten grand. Paid for it in cash, too."

"No way. How did you get it for that?"

"Five finger discount, little man. Now, sit down, shut up, and hold on!" Squidge said as he accelerated quickly, causing the tires to squeal.

Daniel's head pressed against the seat, and he yelled, "Holy crap, this car is fast!"

Squidge let off the gas and said, "Looks like your friends ditched you."

"Yeah, I dunno where they are."

"They left last night after you passed out on the couch."

"Really, they just left me there?"

"Yeah, after I told them they owed me two-hundred bucks for the cocaine."

"Two-hundred!" Daniel said. He placed his hand on his forehead.

"Yeah, they said that you agreed to pay."

"I did . . ." Daniel said as he tried to remember the events prior to making that decision. "Oh yeah, I remember, but I don't have two hundred on me. I have to go to the bank, but I'm only allowed to take out fifty dollars at a time."

"No problem. We'll consider it on credit, I know you're good for it. Do you plan on going back to Tony's next weekend?"

"Yeah!"

"Well, bring the money then and we'll call it even, sound good?"

"Sounds good."

Several minutes after coming to an agreement, Squidge stopped his car outside Daniel's house. He was about to say goodbye, but something caught his eye. He said, "That's a 1962 Ford Falcon. Cherry red, too."

"Yeah, that's my neighbour's car."

"That's my dream car! Who's the grumpy lookin' guy standing next to it?"

"That's Mr. Johnston."

"Gives me the creeps. Better get outta here. See you on Saturday?"

"See you Saturday," Daniel said as he got out of the car. He watched as Squidge revved the engine. He placed it in gear and the tires began squealing so much that smoke engulfed the rear end of the car. Daniel laughed as Squidge sped away but as the smoke cleared, he noticed an unmarked police car parked on the other side of the street. Not giving it a second thought, he turned around and noticed Mr. Johnston standing at the end of his driveway, watching Squidge speed up the hill. He turned around, furrowed his eyebrows, and looked at Daniel without saying anything.

As memories of the weekend were still prevalent, Daniel did not experience a guilty conscience or the need to advise his mother as to his whereabouts. He was, however, exhausted, and as he climbed the stairs to his house, he was reminded of how tired he was. He opened the door and was surprised to see a police officer talking to Marilyn. Upon noticing Daniel, she ran to him and dropped to her knees and started crying. "Thank god, you're home." She wrapped her arms around him and kissed him on the top of his head. Daniel, surprised by the show of affection, stood still and waited until the police officer interrupted.

"Mrs. Harris, seeing that your son has arrived, is there anything else you need from me?"

"No," she said, wiping the tears streaming down her face. "But thank you for everything you've done."

"I'm just glad he's home safe."

"Me too."

Daniel watched through the front window as Marilyn walked the police officer to the sidewalk. Once there, they were approached by Mr. Johnston, who was pointing to the tire marks recently embedded into the street. Daniel watched as the police officer wrote some notes into a small book before getting into his car and driving away in the same direction as Squidge. Halfway up the hill, he turned on his lights and sirens. Daniel would have noticed, but his mother closing the door distracted his attention.

She stood in the doorway, blocking Daniel's escape, and started screaming, "Do you have any idea what I've been through the last two days? Where were you? Why didn't you call home? I had to call the cops. They were about to consider you a missing person! Do you have any idea how this makes me looks like as a parent? Do you even care anymore?"

Daniel, with his head bowed to the floor, said, "No, I don't care anymore and I'm sick and tired of how you treat me. Ever since Dad died, you've been a wreck and you only care about yourself." Daniel raised his voice. "You sleep all day and drink all night. I can't remember the last time you made a meal for me or spent any time with me." He was now yelling. "What did you expect was going to happen? I hate it here and I hate you!"

Daniel approached Marilyn but she did not move. Resolute to leave the living room, he pushed her out of the way, and she fell to the floor. Marilyn clenched her fist, grabbed a shoe, and started hitting Daniel over the head. She grabbed him by the collar and thrust him into the bathroom and said, "Look in the mirror! Tell me what you see."

"No!" Daniel screamed as he threw Marilyn toward the sink, knocking the mirror off the wall. It shattered into a dozen pieces. She found her footing and smacked Daniel with a closed fist on his jaw. Enraged, Daniel grabbed a shard of glass and pressed it to his mother's neck, yelling, "I swear to god I'll kill you!"

Marilyn threw her hands into the air and started crying. Daniel dropped the shard of glass and ran up to his room. He frantically packed a bag with clothing, a toothbrush, soap, and his journal. Moments later, he ran outside, grabbed his bike, and started pedalling as fast as he could. He did not stop until, hours later, he found himself outside Tony Cardinal's house. Mentally and physically exhausted, Daniel knocked on the door and when Tony answered, he started crying.

"What's wrong, little man?" Tony asked.

"I had a fight with my mom. Can I stay here for a few days?"

"You're always welcome here, little man."

# CHAPTER ELEVEN

## A Terrible Idea

Two weeks had passed since Daniel inadvertently sought new dwellings. During that time, both he and Tony enjoyed each other's company as they prepared to harvest the most recent supply of marijuana. Day after day, they could be found sitting in Tony's basement cutting dead leaves, hanging plants to dry, and securing what was ready to be sold in plastic bags. Tony would hide his stash in the ceiling by removing an electrical outlet meant to contain a lightbulb. He would place his arm inside all the way to his shoulder and regularly count the number of bags.

Daniel enjoyed the benefits of assisting Tony and the mind-numbing responsibility of testing the product. He did everything Tony asked of him and never once complained. Daniel would pick up food if Tony was hungry and bring glasses filled with ice that Tony would eat when he was too hot. He would do chores around the house, but the house was too filthy for his efforts to be noticed. Over time, Tony started trusting Daniel and he would reward him with small bags of marijuana. They would get high together and watch hockey and football on the television. However, not all was fun and games at the Cardinal residence.

They spent most of their time inside and Tony always kept the curtains closed. Daniel began noticing Tony's paranoia. He would jump whenever there was a knock at the door, and he never answered his phone. He would always let it go to voicemail. Whenever he heard police sirens, Tony would turn off the lights and tell Daniel to lie down on the floor. Sometimes, without notice, Tony would yell at Daniel if he did something wrong and he would stare with his big, red eyes. He would fill his chest with air and raise his hand as if to strike Daniel. However, he would return to his previous self and was quick to apologize afterwards and say, "I forgot to take my meds today. You know how I get, nothing personal."

The day of the harvest arrived, and Tony was particularly happy. He and Daniel were in the basement sorting the marijuana into bags when Tony, noticing that Daniel's attention was elsewhere, said,

"Don't stop now, little man. We got eleven plants to go. Once were done, we'll celebrate by taking a hit from Big Red."

"Who's Big Red?"

Tony got up and shuffled to the far corner of the basement. The ground was covered with dried stems and leaves. He returned carrying a five-foot-high red cylindrical tube and placed it in front of Daniel. He exclaimed with a smile, "This, my boy, is Big Red."

"What is it?"

"Are you serious? It's the bong! You take one hit off Big Red and you'll be flyin' through space on a rocket ship that looks like a cucumber with pepperoni windows."

Reinvigorated, Daniel regained his focus and continued to fill plastic bags with marijuana. As he gave them to Tony, he watched as Tony placed them in the ceiling. "I've never shown anyone else where I hide my stash. I trust you, little man, but if you ever steal from me, I'll send you to the ICU, got it?" he said, staring at Daniel with wide eyes.

Daniel, now more comfortable around Tony, asked, "Are we friends?"

Tony squinted and said, "Yeah, we're friends. Why?"

"You remind me of someone else I know."

"Why is that?"

"Because he's an Indian, too."

Tony stopped what he was doing and suddenly grabbed Daniel by the shirt and hoisted him off his chair. Daniel, terrorized by the sudden change, could see veins throbbing in Tony's face as he clenched his jaw. His bloodshot eyes widened as he said, "Don't you ever call me that again. Got it?"

"I'm sorry."

"Damn right, you're sorry. If you were anyone else, I'd have removed your head from your shoulders already."

"What did I say, Tony? I didn't mean anything . . ." Daniel said as Tony dumped him back in his chair.

"You're an ignorant piece of white trash, little man. You don't ever call anyone with my heritage an Indian. That's the worst thing you could do."

Daniel, after gaining some courage back, asked, "Why?"

"Because it's a racist term meant to degrade us and remove any sense of history and culture."

"Well, what should I call you?"

"I am First Nations, as in I got here first and everything you see once belonged to my people."

"What happened to it?"

"It was stolen!"

Several minutes passed and nothing was said between them. As tensions decreased, Tony continued, "Don't be a part of the problem, little man. Educate yourself. Learn about the past and what happened to my people and then . . . maybe . . . you'll be part of the solution."

"But—"

"I don't wanna talk about it anymore. It just gets me angry, and I don't want to not be in a good mood because we're almost done here."

They continued pruning. Daniel, wanting to change the subject, asked, "How did you get your scar?"

"You really don't want me to enjoy myself, do you? If you must know, I got this after my uncle drove over my head with his truck. I was babysitting my cousin. We were wrestling and when I threw him onto the bed, he hit his head against the wall. Later that night, he fell asleep and never got up. In the morning, I found my cousin dead. After I told my uncle, he beat me up and put my head behind the rear wheel of his truck. He drove over my head and several days later I woke up in the hospital. Since then, I've had three strokes and I suffer from post-traumatic stress, depression, anxiety, you name it! All this time I've tried not to think about it and now, in the last three minutes, I've had to relive the worst parts of my life." The longer Tony spoke, the louder his voice became. He stood up and let out a resounding yell that reverberated in Daniel's chest. He shuffled toward Daniel. Thinking he was going to struck, Daniel flinched as Tony reached for Big Red and placed it in between them. "A little edgy are ya, little man?"

"Um . . . yeah."

"Well, then I think it's time we celebrated a little early." Tony stuffed a small silver bowl on the side of Big Red with marijuana. Daniel watched as he lit the end and started to inhale. The cylinder filled with smoke. Tony placed his thumb over a small hole at the top and demanded, "Take a hit, champ!"

Without hesitation, Daniel placed his lips over the hole and inhaled the contents of Big Red. He was about to cough when Tony violently placed his hands over his mouth and nose while yelling, "Don't you dare!" He lifted Daniel by the head and placed him over a sink in the corner of the basement. Daniel clung to the sides as his arms shook. Tony let go and plumes of smoke escaped from Daniel's mouth and nose. He coughed violently and bent over the sink, fighting the urge to vomit while Tony laughed.

It took several minutes to regain his composure, but when he did, Daniel experienced a sense of euphoria he did not know was possible. He was overcome with a sense of happiness, and he started laughing. He looked around him as the room began to swirl. He could not walk in a straight line, and he ended up tripping over an exposed pot and falling to the ground. Lying there, Daniel circulated the room with his eyes as the sense of ecstasy continued. He could hear Tony laughing before taking his turn on Big Red. Moments later, the two of them were rolling around on the floor, laughing and hugging each other; any sense of the previous transgressions dissipated with the smoke evaporating from their lungs.

"Isn't Big Red the greatest?" Tony asked, the laughter now dulled.

"Big Red is the greatest," Daniel agreed as they stumbled upstairs. He lay down on the living room floor as Tony sat on the couch. The room continued to spin. There were a few remaining fits of laughter until, ten minutes later, both Tony and Daniel fell asleep. They did not move, and as they drifted off into a world of intoxicated delight, they were able to ignore the tragedy of life.

As Tony and Daniel were enjoying the reprieve from thoughts of the past, Marilyn sought refuge from her reflections by punishing her body with another cocktail of whiskey and Xanax. She had heard, through rumours, of Daniel's whereabouts and the concerns she once had for her son were eclipsed by the incessant need to consume alcohol.

This continued for the next two years as both mother and son, consumed by their own addictions, succumbed to the grip of continual yet temporary narcosis and never once realized that they had more in common than they did not. Their reluctance towards self-improvement caused a downward spiral. They ignored pleas from family and friends and showed no intention to begin the healing process. As time passed, both Daniel and Marilyn were left to their own devices; those who had tried to help clung to hope that their loved ones would eventually choose to get better.

It was shortly after Daniel's sixteenth birthday when he found himself, Josh, Tom, and Gary on the corner of Clifton Hill and Victoria Street. Surrounded by the lights and the noise of limitless forms of entertainment, they looked upon the thousands of tourists that flocked to this area of Niagara Falls with monetary delight. Supplied by Tony Cardinal with an abundance of marijuana, they divided into two teams and walked on each side of the street, looking for anyone who wanted to buy drugs. They could rely on the usual purchasers and by the time they reached the Niagara Parkway, their pockets were lined with cash. They got high while overlooking the Niagara River before walking up Clifton Hill and stopping at their favourite spots for food and viewing pleasure.

They were enjoying their meal, sitting on the street-level patio of Burger King. Daniel was about to dig into his fries when Josh brought up a topic of conversation they had discussed in the past. "I really do think we should go into business for ourselves," he said.

"Oh, not again," Tom said.

"Yeah, not again," Gary added.

Daniel remained silent as he consumed the remainder of his dinner.

"Oh, come on, guys. I've done the math. We could make an extra two thousand bucks each if we grew our own stash. If we grew three crops per year, that's an extra six thousand per year."

"I don't know," Tom whined. "Tony's treated us surprisingly good. And we don't even know how to look after a tulip. How would we grow a crop of marijuana? We need supplies. We need a place to grow."

"I've been thinkin'," Josh continued, "There's a place on Morrison for rent. Big house with a big basement. We could go in together and Daniel knows how to grow. He's helped Tony with every crop the past two years. He could do it with his eyes closed."

"You think so?" Tom asked as he looked at Daniel. Josh and Gary did the same.

"Yeah, but it would cost a lot of money to get it up and running."

"Well, hot damn," Josh said, "I think we're gonna be in business. How much do you think we'll need to start?"

"At least a thousand."

"Okay, so a thousand for equipment, plus another fifteen hundred for rent—"

"I think you mean three thousand for rent," Tom interrupted.

"Huh?"

"First and last up-front equals three thousand, plus one thousand for supplies. Also add another thousand for food, furniture, electricity, water. It's gonna take a year to save up that much cash."

Tom's realistic approach stunted Josh's idealized vision. However, he did not let any hurdles stand in his way. He suggested, "We could steal Tony's stash."

Daniel spat out the pop he was drinking through a straw and said, "Are you crazy? Tony would kill us if we stole from him. He'd beat the crap outta us if he knew we were having this conversation."

"No, not all of it. Just enough to cover the up-front cost. Think about it, guys," Josh continued. "There's a big party at his place tonight. We could take it then. Daniel knows where he hides his stash, right?"

Daniel hesitated but reluctantly said, "Yeah" as his friends looked at him with reinvigorated enthusiasm. "But there's no way I'm gonna take it."

"I'll do it," Josh said. "Just tell me where it is, and I'll grab it. You can be next to Tony the entire party. That way he'll never believe that you took it."

"Actually, it sounds like a good plan," Tom said.

"I think it's a terrible idea," Daniel said.

After receiving reassurances from his friends that the heist would go off without a hitch, Daniel succumbed to their naive rationale and told Josh where Tony hid his stash of marijuana. They bounded to their feet and began walking up Clifton Hill.

They had made it halfway up the street when Daniel saw a girl who looked familiar. He looked a second time but this time her back was facing him. He approached, and as his hormones started pulsating through his body, Daniel said, "Excuse me."

She stood up straight, turned around, and said, "Oh my god . . . Daniel Harris! I haven't seen you in forever. I miss you."

"Olivia?" Daniel said, shocked by how beautiful she had become. She was just as tall as he was, and her piercing amber eyes looked directly into his. Her dimpled smile lit up her face and she smelled like cotton candy. Olivia hugged him, and it was the first time in years he experienced such warmth and compassion. He wished to remain in her arms, but the two were interrupted when someone said, "What the heck is going on here?"

Daniel saw a six-foot-tall blond-haired teenager walking toward them. He was wearing a white T-shirt and blue jeans, his broad shoulders and muscular stature intimidating Daniel.

"Chris, this is Daniel. My old friend I told you about," Olivia said with a wide smile.

"Hey," Chris snarled, the jealousy oozing from his pores. "The drug dealer, right? Anyways, we gonna go or what?" he said as he took Olivia by the wrist.

"I'm sorry, Daniel, but I gotta go. It was good to see you. Drop by the house sometime," Olivia said before giving him one more hug goodbye.

Daniel watched as Olivia and Chris waited in line for the Ripley's Believe It or Not museum. They started kissing each other and the display angered him. Olivia's presence provoked a surge of traumatic memories he had tried so hard to ignore. Daniel desperately tried to remain in the present, but he was overcome with emotion and sat down with his head between his knees.

He felt a hand grab his shoulder. He assumed it was Josh, but when he looked up, Olivia was standing in front of him. He stammered and his voice became raspy.

"I couldn't just leave you like that," Olivia said as she sat next to Daniel. "I haven't seen you in years."

"What about your boyfriend?" Daniel asked with a jealous glare.

"Enough of that, Daniel. What did you expect? Suddenly you run away from home and the next thing I hear is that you're selling drugs. I couldn't believe it."

"Well, believe it."

"What happened to you? Why did you run away?"

"I don't wanna talk about it, Olivia," Daniel said. He stood up and took several paces. He turned around and Olivia was next to him.

"Well, you need to talk about it and I'm the best person to talk to."

"Why is that?"

"Have you forgotten, Daniel?" Olivia exclaimed. Those nearest to them turned around to see what was happening. "I loved you. I still love you and I want you to come home. Your mother needs you."

"Don't get me started on my mother," Daniel said as he began walking away. Olivia matched his pace.

"When was the last time you saw her? She's not doing well. She gets weaker every day and just last week she fell down the stairs and broke her ankle."

"I really don't care about my mom anymore. Just leave me alone, okay."

Olivia stopped as Daniel continued walking. He was amongst a crowd of people when he heard her yell, "I'll never stop caring about you. Maybe you should start caring about yourself!"

Daniel increased his pace until he met up with Josh, Tom, and Gary at the top of Clifton Hill. They asked him what took so long but he blamed it on the tourists. He tried to forget what happened, but the thought of Olivia haunted him until they arrived at Tony's house.

They were a block away when they heard music blaring from his stereo system. The street was filled with cars and the chaotic noise of conversations echoing in the backyard. They bounded up the stairs but before entering, Daniel experienced an upsetting sensation in his stomach. He said, "Hey, guys. I really don't think stealing from Tony is a good idea. I got a bad feeling about it."

"Oh, I'm so glad you said something," Tom said. "I don't wanna steal from Tony either. Can we call it off?"

"Yeah, let's call it off," Gary added. The three of them looked at Josh.

Josh put up his hands and said, "Okay, all right, you wimps. We'll call it off. But just for the record, you're a bunch of pansies."

"I don't care what you call us, Josh. It was a bad idea in the first place," Daniel said. "I just wanna enjoy the party. Is that too much to ask?"

"Hell, no!" Josh replied. "Let's party!"

Relieved that the heist was called off, Daniel, Tom, Gary, and Josh entered the house and were promptly greeted by Tony. He was happy to see them and, as usual, there was a plethora of drugs and alcohol to choose from. As they careened between rooms, their inebriated state increased, and by the time midnight arrived they were no longer lucid.

Two hours later, Tony found Daniel passed out on the couch. He picked him up with one arm, threw him over his shoulders, and spun him around in circles. He threw him on the floor, and Daniel ran to and stuck his head out the nearest window. Moments later, he vomited the contents of his stomach. When he returned, he was surprised by what he saw. "Squidge, is that you?"

"You're damn right, it's me. I got out a month ago," Squidge said as he picked up Daniel and shook him. Daniel felt sick again but there was nothing left in his stomach.

"Got outta where?" Daniel slurred.

"Seriously, I've been gone for two years, and you didn't notice? I've been in jail, little man. Remember that night I drove you home?"

"That was two years ago?" Daniel asked, surprised.

"Time flies, I know. After I dropped you off, I got pulled over a few blocks from your home. The cops searched my car and found my stash of cocaine in the trunk. I got charged with intent to sell."

"Sorry to hear that."

"Me too. You owe me, remember?"

"Owe you what?"

"Two hundred bucks," Squidge said as he extended his hand.

Daniel reached into his pocket and produced the two hundred dollars he owed Squidge.

"Fantastic!" he exclaimed as he escorted Daniel into the kitchen. "It looks like you need a little pick-me-up. You wanna take a bump?"

Daniel accepted Squidge's proposal and inhaled a small amount of cocaine. He immediately perked up; he had forgotten how much he enjoyed its effects. With his energy restored, he, Squidge, and Tony drank, smoked, and partied until dawn.

They slept the afternoon away until Daniel was suddenly awakened by the sound of Tony yelling, "Where is it? Where is it, you little—" He grabbed Daniel's shirt and slapped his face.

Daniel, now completely awake and terrified, said, "Where's what?"

Tony struck him in the face again and said, "You're the only person who knows where I keep my stash." He punched him in the stomach and repeated, "Where is it?"

"I have no idea what you mean," Daniel groaned, now lying in the fetal position on the floor. Squidge came into the room and said, "What's going on?"

"One bag is missing. A five-pound bag worth twenty-five hundred bucks is gone! Where is it, little man?" Tony exclaimed as he continued to kick Daniel in the face.

Enraged, Tony continued the onslaught of physical violence. Squidge tried to pull him off but was unable. Tony knelt on Daniel's chest and kept hitting him in the face until he was out of breath. He then grabbed Daniel by the ankle and dragged him outside. He threw him on the grass and yelled, "You've got two options. Get me the bag or get me the money. You've got two weeks. Don't even think about comin' around here if you don't have nothin'."

Tony went inside. Squidge picked up Daniel; he groaned in pain as his bruised and bloodied face swelled. He was taken to the hospital where his injuries were tended to. The doctor attempted to find the source of the injuries, but Daniel did not say a word. He did not wait around to be discharged and Squidge took him to his apartment to rest. He looked after Daniel for two days until he was coherent enough to eat and drink on his own. Seated against the wall, Daniel delicately touched the areas of his face that were either stitched or bruised and when he was done, he looked at Squidge and asked, "What do I do now?"

Squidge stroked his chin with his finger and said, "Tony's loss is my gain."

# CHAPTER TWELVE

# A Debt Paid

Daniel was cursing Josh Thompson's name as thoughts of vengeance circulated in his mind. However, not being a vengeful person, nor incapable of inciting violence toward another, his opinions remained within, accompanying a multitude of similar feelings that had compiled since his father's death.

He was sitting at the kitchen table in Squidge's apartment. For the first time in three days, Daniel was able to open his swollen eyes. He looked around and was surprised by how clean it was. Everything had its place and every surface reflected light. The remainder of the apartment was just as tidy and as Daniel entered the living room, he recognized the newest Nintendo 64 gaming console. He grabbed the controller and traced its edges with his thumbs. He turned it on and started playing Mario Kart. Entranced by the game, Daniel did not notice Squidge watching him from the hallway. "It's one of the first gaming systems to use a sixty-four-bit processor. Way better than the previous model," he said.

Squidge watched Daniel play. It was a welcome escape from reality, but that quickly changed when Squidge asked, "So, what are you gonna do about Tony?"

Daniel sighed. "I have no idea."

"Well, I got an idea. How 'bout you start sellin' for me?"

"Sell? Sell what?"

"Cocaine."

Daniel paused the game, placed the controller on his lap, and looked at Squidge with a raised eyebrow. "Really? You want me to sell cocaine?"

"Yeah, unless you have a better idea how to get back the twenty-five hundred bucks you own Tony. There's a lot of things in life I would do, but the one thing that tops my list of things I *wouldn't* do is owe Tony money. He's like an animal sometimes. Just look at your face."

"Yeah, but I never thought it would happen to me. The worst thing I saw happened about a year ago. This guy, Dino Guido, lost a couple hundred dollars' worth of marijuana. Said he tossed it out the car because the cops were chasing him. Tony didn't believe him and locked him in the basement for a week until a buddy of Dino's promised to pay what he owed."

"That was over a couple hundred bucks, eh? Well, what do you think Tony would do to you for twenty-five hundred? You know he took it easy on you because he liked you. You got lucky, little man."

"I know," Daniel said as he gently touched the swollen areas of his face. "But I don't have that much money. It would take me a month or two to get it back, but Tony only gave me two weeks."

"I could front you the money."

"Really?" Daniel exclaimed, breathing a sigh of relief.

"Yeah, if you start sellin' for me, you could make twenty-five hundred in a few days . . ."

"A few days?"

"Yeah, I've got a shipment arriving next week. We'll go over to Tony's today and pay him back. Then next week you help me prep the batch for sale and hit the streets. I'll show you around to all my contacts. We'll make a killing, you and me!"

Daniel hesitated at the thought of going back to Tony's. The physical and mental trauma from when he last saw Tony gave him nightmares and he was constantly looking over his shoulder whenever there was a loud sound. However, as Squidge continued to explain his scenario, Daniel accepted his proposal.

Later that afternoon, they went over to Tony Cardinal's place and paid him the money Daniel owed. He invited them inside and his demeanour changed once he had the cash in hand. Daniel remained silent and looked around nervously. His knees shook and with every passing minute he became more eager to leave, but Tony insisted they stay for a while.

"You look a little nervous, little man. Can't understand why." Tony laughed. He stared at Daniel with bloodshot eyes and said, "Nothing personal, little man. It was just business. I can't go around having people think I'm soft. Anyways, Squidge tells me you're gonna be sellin' for him now, is that right? Movin' up in the world, eh. Little man thinks he's gonna take over the city, don't cha?"

"Yeah, I guess," Daniel said, hoping they would be permitted to leave soon.

"I don't think you do. I'm going to tell you a story my dad once told me," Tony said, now sitting on the edge of his seat. "A long time ago, in a lush green forest that covered the countryside, stood a tree. It was just like every other tree in the forest until, one day, there was a raging fire that destroyed the entire forest, but the tree survived. It grew, and grew, and grew. It grew so big that its shadow covered the forest, and the other trees couldn't grow because the sunshine was blocked. The other trees were scared because they were so small, and they didn't want to anger the massive tree. On it went for hundreds of years until, one day, there was a storm. The wind blew the massive tree over because its roots weren't strong enough. It fell and shattered into a thousand pieces. The day after, there was a bright blue sky and finally the entire forest received the sunlight that had been blocked for so long."

Daniel looked at Tony with a scrunched face and said, "I don't get it."

"You will one day," Tony said as he showed Daniel and Squidge to the door. He surprised Daniel by wrapping his arms around his waist and lifting him off the floor. He squeezed and said, "You were my favourite, little man, but I don't trust you anymore. Too bad your friend messed everything up."

Daniel turned around and was about to leave when Tony grabbed his shirt and spun him around. Daniel cringed, thinking he was about to be struck, but instead Tony threw a duffle bag at his chest. "This is your stuff, little man. Including that stupid journal of yours. I couldn't help but look . . . Boy, you sure got some mommy issues, don't cha?" Tony laughed again as he slammed the door in Daniel's face.

Squidge remained silent because he wanted to leave as quickly as Daniel did. They were about to get into his car when Tony yelled, "By the way. I heard Josh was in Toronto tryin' to sell what he stole. If you see him first, tell him to leave the country because if I get my hands on him, I'm gonna kill 'em."

Daniel shrugged and took his place in the passenger seat. He was concerned about Josh and what Tony promised he would do to him. "Do you think we should warn Josh?"

"You kidding me? After what he did to you, Josh deserves whatever Tony is gonna do to him."

"He said he's gonna kill him."

"Oh, he's just blowin' smoke up your butt. He's not going to kill Josh. He'll beat him up, but Tony isn't stupid enough to kill someone."

"If you say so."

Daniel rolled down the window and felt the rush of wind in between his fingers as they returned to Squidge's apartment. He remained there, enjoying the daily routine of playing video games and eating fast food.

The only thing that tainted his experience was that Daniel had gone several days without drugs or alcohol. He experienced nausea and would sweat during the night, and he noticed his hands would shake the longer he held on to the controller. He felt tired most of the time and it was during this desperate episode when he asked Squidge, "Can we do a line?"

Squidge looked at Daniel with a stern face and said, "Never do cocaine from your own stash."

"Why? I used to see you do it all the time at Tony's parties."

"Yeah, because he paid for it. I'll do it if someone else is payin'. It's the first rule in this business. Don't take from your own supply or else you'll end up owing more than you got. Look, if you can wait until tomorrow, I usually do a couple lines after prepping the shipment."

"Really? Awesome."

"But don't get too excited, little man. I don't throw big parties like Tony does. I don't wanna create that much attention."

"What do you mean?"

"I'm still on parole. If I get caught with possession, I could go back to jail for a long time. That's why you're here. You're only sixteen, so if you get caught, you'll only get community service or something like that."

Squidge spent the remainder of the day educating Daniel about the rules of purchasing and selling cocaine. Daniel did his best to understand, but his cravings didn't allow him to focus for long. Eventually, the only thing he could think about was the cocaine he would get the following evening.

As instructed, Daniel waited in the foyer of the Econo Lodge on Victoria Avenue. No one noticed him among the surplus of tourists. It was not long until a black truck arrived. Daniel recognized the licence plate and got inside. He nervously looked at the driver and noticed he was dressed in black. The driver remained silent as he gripped the steering wheel and began driving. Daniel was surprised when someone from the back seat grabbed his shoulder and tossed a small black bag onto his lap. He grabbed a thick envelope from Daniel and started counting the money within; Daniel heard the sound of bills being folded and a thumb being licked. Silence remained as they drove down Victoria Avenue as it turned into Ferry Street. After an "Okay" there was a sharp turn into the parking lot next to a liquor store.

The truck stopped and Daniel got out. He waited until he was able to flag down a taxi and instructed the driver where to take him. They stopped a block away from Squidge's apartment. Daniel walked at a hurried pace, looking over his shoulder. His anxieties did not recede until he was in the apartment building. He knocked on the door and Squidge, with a smile on his face, answered and said, "Congratulations, little man, you busted your cocaine cherry."

Daniel breathed a sigh of relief and said, "That was the scariest thing I've ever done."

Squidge took the bag from Daniel and opened it on the kitchen table. "You see this," he said, placing three brick-sized, plastic, duct-taped containers into his hands. "Do you have any idea how much we can sell this for?"

"No."

"Fourteen thousand dollars!" Squidge exclaimed. "And it's all thanks to you, little man."

Daniel, sharing in the excitement, watched as Squidge began opening each package. He dumped the contents into a large stainless-steel bowl. He pointed to the counter and said, "You see that box over there?"

"Yeah," Daniel said as he investigated the box and noticed a dozen white bottles. "What's in these?"

"Those are caffeine pills. I need you to grind them up and then we'll mix them with the cocaine."

"Why?"

"Because we can turn three pounds of cocaine into four pounds of cocaine. Understand? Now stop asking questions and do what I need you to do."

Daniel did as instructed, and before midnight they had prepared every last ounce of cocaine. They sighed collectively and Daniel was excited when Squidge said, "Let's do a line or two."

Daniel watched in earnest anticipation and did not hesitate to indulge when it was his turn. He felt the surge of energy as the drugs bombarded his system. He enjoyed the high as the effects of the cocaine masked the memories and emotions associated with sobriety. They remained awake the rest of the night, playing video games and eating pizza. It was not until dawn when the necessity of sleep overcame any amount of cocaine they could ingest.

Daniel awoke several hours later when he heard Squidge talking on the phone. Darkness had returned and he was surprised to have slept the day away. Moments later, he was being dragged to his feet before they scurried around Niagara Falls. They made several stops, mostly in dark alleys and derelict houses and apartments. Daniel was responsible for distributing the cocaine as Squidge counted the money. The excitement of each transaction overcame any thoughts of illegality and when they arrived back at Squidge's apartment with a bag full of cash, the sensation of joy increased with every dollar they counted.

This went on for several months. As their success increased, so did Daniel's reliability on cocaine. As he continued to use, he became easily panicked and suffered from visual hallucinations of his father lying in his coffin, of his mother pushing his face into a mirror, and of Tony standing over him, staring with his bloodshot eyes.

Before long, the only comfort Daniel achieved was in consuming cocaine. He disregarded Squidge's advice and began taking from his own stash, and as his addiction increased so did the amount of cocaine he was inhaling. Two months had passed and in his continually euphoric state, he lost track of his finances. Finally, Squidge brought it to his attention that Daniel owed him for what he was using.

"How much do I owe you again?" Daniel said.

"Ten thousand dollars." Squidge grinned.

"Ten thousand! When— How?" Daniel said frantically, his eyes dilated.

"I told you not to use from your own stash, little man. It adds up quick!"

"Where am I gonna get ten grand from?"

"I have it."

"You do? Well, help me out. You've done it before, do it again," Daniel demanded.

"You'll get nothing if you talk to me that way. But lucky for you, I'm willing to give it to you if—"

"Yeah, if what?"

"If you get me that cherry of a car your old neighbour has."

"Mr. Johnston?"

"Yeah, he has a 1962 Ford Falcon. My favourite car, as it happens to be. If you can get me that car, I will forgive your debt."

Daniel ruminated for several minutes, struggling with thoughts of loyalty toward his former neighbour. He paced throughout Squidge's apartment, talking to himself. "Okay, I owe ten grand and I don't have any drugs to sell. So, where am I going to get the money? Maybe I can get it from Tony? No, don't be stupid. That's a horrible idea. Maybe I could ask my mom? No, that's even worse. Oh, I can't think straight. What the hell is happening to me? Okay, maybe we could steal his car. I mean, I know where he hides the extra key to his back door. And he always places the keys to the Falcon on the hook."

Daniel finally stopped, looked at Squidge, and said, "I'll do it!"

"Great!" Squidge pumped his fist. "We'll leave after midnight."

"What? Tonight?"

"Yeah, unless you want me to start charging interest."

Daniel started hyperventilating and it took him several minutes to calm down. He accepted the reality of the situation, and both he and Squidge went over the plan of how to escape unseen.

Several hours later, under the cover of darkness, they drove past Mr. Johnston's house; their confidence increased upon noticing that no lights were on inside. Squidge parked his car two blocks away, underneath a large maple tree that covered the light emanating from the streetlamp. He gave the keys to Daniel as they walked past his childhood home. A wave of memories crashed over Daniel, none of which were happy. He clenched his jaw and felt the pressure increase in his head.

They waited in the darkness and scoured their surroundings for movement, but there was none. They snuck up the driveway with their backs against Mr. Johnston's house. Daniel noticed the living room light was on in his old house.

He stopped and approached the window. He peered inside and saw a mess of empty alcohol bottles and takeout food containers. The floor was covered in dirt and old clothing. Sections of paint had been removed from the baseboards and entire segments of wallpaper had somehow been stripped off. Daniel saw a shadow approaching, so he quickly ducked out of the way. It moved slowly as if it hobbled. Curious, Daniel looked within and watched as his mother laid down on the couch.

He was shocked to see how frail she was. She had a large cast covering her lower left leg and she used a cane as she adjusted herself. Her skin was pale. Her hair was riddled with stands of white and it looked as if it had not been combed in days. For a moment, Daniel felt sympathetic toward his mother. He looked upon her with remorse, but it was not long until traumatic memories changed that feeling to hatred and resentment.

Squidge pulled Daniel away from the window. They knelt next to Mr. Johnston's back door and searched for a magnetic key box Daniel knew to be there. It did not take them long to locate it underneath a large flowerpot. A moment of doubt overcame Daniel, but the need to repay his debt surmounted any thoughts of uncertainty. Without making a sound, Daniel opened the back door and took the key to Mr. Johnston's prized possession off the hook. They opened the garage door manually, turned on the ignition, and put the car into neutral. They pushed the car down the driveway and onto the street.

Once they were far enough away from the house, Squidge jumped inside, popped the clutch, and sped away into the darkness. Daniel ran as fast as he could to where Squidge parked his car. Sweating profusely, he put the car into drive and headed toward Niagara Falls. He caught up to Squidge and followed him to a self-storage garage on Taylor Road. After securing the car, they shared a unanimous breath of relief before returning to Squidge's apartment.

"Can you believe it?" Squidge said. "I finally have a 1962 Ford Falcon. We must celebrate! You did amazing, little man," he said, patting Daniel on the back.

"What are you gonna do with it? You can't just drive it around."

"Not to worry. I got a buddy of mine coming down in a few days. He's got a shop in Thorold. We're going to paint it black and change the rims and tires. Your old neighbour won't even recognize it."

"And you're gonna forgive what I owe, right?"

"Oh yeah, and I got a special treat tonight to celebrate," Squidge said as they arrived at his apartment.

"What is it?"

"It's a surprise."

Wanting to alleviate himself from his feelings of guilt, Daniel accepted Squidge's gift and watched as he mixed several lines of cocaine with another substance unknown to him.

"What's that you're adding to it?"

"It's something special I keep for occasions like this. I'll go first," Squidge said as he inhaled quickly. "Your turn." He placed a rolled-up five-dollar bill in Daniel's hand.

Daniel gave into peer pressure and followed suit, snorting the two lines in front of him; Squidge laughed as he inhaled.

Within minutes, Daniel was experiencing a high like never before. He was extremely happy and was subject to bouts of laughter. However, the pleasant effects of the drug diminished, and a sense of worry came over him. "Something's happening," Daniel exclaimed. "Why are my fingers moving like that? Why do I have four sets of hands? Why am I floating? I don't like this!"

"You're in the K-hole now, little man." Squidge laughed.

"K-hole? I don't wanna be in a hole."

"Too late. Welcome to the wonderful world of Special K."

Squidge was referring to a powerful hallucinogenic. Daniel's panic increased as he experienced visions of his deceased father walking toward him. He locked himself in the bathroom. He felt safe until he saw his reflection in the mirror and felt his mother's breath on the back of his neck. He shattered the glass with his fist. Blood started oozing from his wrist. He covered the wound with his other hand and ran out of Squidge's apartment. His lungs burned with exhaustion as he sprinted down the street, his father's ghost chasing him. Squidge's pleas for him to calm down went unnoticed.

Daniel's heart pounded as the hallucinogenic properties of the drug increased. He felt like he was flying, moving at incredible speeds as tracers of light were all around him. Daniel eventually collapsed in a parking lot next to the Skylon Tower. He crawled toward a public bathroom and remained there, lying on the floor. He went in and out of consciousness as blood drained from the gash on his wrist. Daniel saw a large shadow standing over him and just before he passed out, he felt his body being lifted off the floor.

# CHAPTER THIRTEEN

## A Guardian Angel

Daniel woke up in the hospital. He noticed a bag of saline hanging above him and followed the tube to where it punctured his skin. He saw that his wrist was covered with a bandage partially consumed with blood. He tried to adjust himself, but the slightest movement caused him pain. Daniel grunted and his sound of discomfort aroused Dr. Fitzgerald's attention. Daniel did not see him resting in the chair across from his bed as his eyes adjusted to the light.

"You're lucky to be here," Dr. Fitzgerald said as he looked over Daniel. "I think you have a guardian angel."

"What do you mean?" Daniel said, his voice strained.

"Five minutes! Five more minutes, and we would have lost you," Dr. Fitzgerald said. He sat next to Daniel on the bed and delicately grabbed his bandaged wrist. "When he brought you here, you had lost so much blood that the nurses had a heck of time trying to find your vein."

"Who brought me here?"

"Peter Michaels."

"Who is that?"

"I think your friends call him Peanut Butter Pete. Did you know he used to be a cop? I think he was your father's partner for a while."

"Really? Peanut Butter Pete brought me here?" Daniel exclaimed, but his sudden movement caused a sharp pain to travel through his body.

"Try to settle down, Daniel. Your body has been through a lot. Did you know that's the second time Peter saved your life?"

"The second?"

"Remember when you bumped your head jumping off the old canal?"

"Yeah," Daniel said. He touched the back of his head where his scar was.

"Well, guess who saved you from the water?"

"Oh yeah, I forgot. For some reason I thought it was Josh or Tom that pulled me out of the water."

"Nope. It was me," Pete said from the doorway. Daniel did not recognize him because he was clean shaven, and his hair had been cut short. He was wearing new denim jeans and a long-sleeved shirt. He approached Daniel and stood next to him.

"You look so . . . clean," Daniel said as Dr. Fitzgerald adjusted his bed upright before excusing himself.

Pete sat in a chair next to Daniel and said, "They take good care of me here. Every once in a while, I come by for a check-up and they let me take a shower and give me clean clothing and a hot meal. I wanted to drop by to see how you were doing. Looks like they got you patched up. How are you feeling?"

"I'm dizzy and my wrist hurts," Daniel said.

"Here, I brought you this," Pete said and gave Daniel a pre-wrapped peanut butter and strawberry jam sandwich. "You lost a lot of blood. You'll begin to feel better after eating something."

"I guess I should thank you for saving my life . . . two times," Daniel said in between bites. "Dr. Fitzgerald said you were a cop, too. He said you were my dad's partner."

"That's right. I was a cop for about ten years. I was your dad's partner when your mother was pregnant with you. He used to talk about how he excited he was to be a dad. They knew you were going to be a boy, so Keith used to tell me about how he was going to play catch with you, take you camping, and teach you how to ride a bike." He noticed a tear collecting in Daniel's eye. "I'm really sorry about what happened to your father. He was a great guy and he always looked after me. Especially when I . . ."

"When what?" Daniel said as Pete's chin quivered.

"After I left the Niagara regional police."

"Why did you stop being a cop?"

"It's a sad story. Are you sure you want to hear it?"

"Yeah."

"It was shortly after you were born. Your dad and I were responding to a vehicle collision on the 406 where it merges onto the Q.E. A massive thunderstorm had rolled through, so the road was covered with water. The car lost control and struck a support beam. The car was nearly torn in half. When I approached, I recognized that it was my wife's car. I looked inside and saw . . ." Pete grabbed a tissue from his pocket and wiped his eyes.

"Saw what?"

"My wife and daughter inside the car. The impact killed them both immediately."

Silence consumed them as they were both lost in grief. Several minutes later, Pete said, "I was devastated by the loss of my wife and daughter. I couldn't work. I was depressed. I lost weight and at my lowest point, I attempted suicide."

"You tried to kill yourself?"

"Yes, and you know what happened?"

"No."

"I'll remember this for the rest of my life. Your dad was on patrol. He found me in my car in the garage while doing a welfare check. I had secured a hose to the exhaust and filled my car with carbon monoxide. I was unconscious when he pulled me out. I came to in the back of the ambulance. Your father was next to me. I was frantic and trying to understand what was going on when he grabbed my wrist and said, 'There's still life left to be lived.' His words were like a revelation to me. For the first time since their death, I wanted to get better. I remained here, in the hospital, for a few months afterward. I started talking with a psychiatrist and during therapy I realized, after surviving my attempted suicide, that I appreciated life. Since then, I've continued to get better. I still have a long way to go. I know I'm going to have difficult days, but at least they don't happen all the time now. Most of my days are good days now and as I continue to get better, I will always have your father to thank for saving my life. And you know what the crazy thing is?"

"What?"

"If your dad didn't save me, I wouldn't have been around to save you . . . twice."

This fateful moment resounded within Daniel's mind. He thought about all the nuances of his childhood and imagined if anything would have been different—how it would have had a drastic effect on his life.

"Your father was my guardian angel, Daniel—"

"And it sounds like Peter is yours," a familiar voice said from behind the door. It opened to reveal Uncle Ross and Wade. They approached Daniel and gave him a hug and expressed their gratefulness to Pete. Their compassion allowed Daniel's mind a reprieve from the onslaught of questions regarding his whereabouts.

They made him laugh and explained how happy they were that he was alive.

"We left as soon as Dr. Fitzgerald told us you were in the hospital," Wade said.

"It's a six-hour drive from Algonquin Park," Daniel stated. "How did you get down here so fast?"

"You've been here for two days," Dr. Fitzgerald said as he entered the room.

"Two days," Daniel said as he scratched his head, searching for a memory. Concerned for his own well-being, Daniel struggled with the decision to divulge the information he had. However, after listening to Pete's story and feeling a crushing sense of remorse, Daniel propped himself up and frantically said, "There's still time!"

"Time for what?" Wade said.

"To get Mr. Johnston's car back."

Daniel told everyone what had led to his admittance to the hospital. Pete called the police and explained where Mr. Johnston's car was. They arrived just as Squidge and an associate of his were loading it onto an enclosed truck. They arrested both and found several ounces of cocaine after searching Squidge's apartment.

Later that day, the police arrived at the hospital and gave Daniel his duffle bag. He removed the stale clothing and found his journal amongst some dirty socks. Comprehending the possibility of incarceration, Daniel was relieved when the police told him that Mr. Johnston would not press charges against him. Additionally, many officers had sympathy for him because they had known Keith, and Daniel had to promise to commit to a drug recovery program.

"Where will I stay? I'm not ready to go home and deal with my mom yet," Daniel said.

"Your mom has . . . recently moved," Ross said.

"Marilyn had another fall, Daniel, and she's been taken to a residence that will help her look after herself," Wade added in a soft voice.

"Where is my mom? What's going to happen with the house?"

"I think that's a discussion better left for another time," Ross commented. "Perhaps, in a week or two when you're feeling well, we'll talk about your mom."

"For the meantime," Wade added, "We're going to take you back to our place for a while."

"Would you like that?" Dr. Fitzgerald asked.

"Yes, very much. I've wanted to live with Uncle Ross and Wade for a long time," Daniel said with a smile.

Daniel was discharged from the hospital the following day. He was treated to lunch at McDonald's before the long drive. Along the way, he had plenty of time to think about what happened—the bandage on his wrist was a constant reminder. He thought about Pete and hoped to see him again. As they drove, the skyscrapers of Toronto descended beyond the horizon, and the bustle of a busy highway turned into green countryside. They stopped in Barrie for a snack and fuelled up the car. It was getting dark, and the ability to observe the passing countryside faded with the sunlight. In the darkness, Daniel was haunted by glimpses of Tony standing over him and blood pulsating from his wrist as he lay on the bathroom floor. Wade extended his hand and said, "We'll be there in less than an hour."

It was pitch black when they arrived; the sound of crunching gravel was the only thing guiding their way to the front door. Wade showed Daniel to his room while Ross started a fire. The warmth from the flames filled the room by the time they came downstairs.

"Who's hungry?" Ross asked to which Wade and Daniel replied, "I am."

"Join me outside while we wait for dinner," Wade said. He escorted Daniel to the nearest dock. It brought back fond memories of their fishing expeditions. He tilted his head back and was absorbed by the number of stars and how bright they were.

"Welcome back," Wade said as he wrapped his arm around Daniel's shoulder. "I'm glad you're here."

"Me too." Daniel smiled.

"Are you ready to commit to getting better?"

"Yes, I think so."

"Can I tell you something my father once told me?"

"Sure."

"There's a pathway leading to a journey within placed before you. The man who looks at his feet will get lost the farther he walks. And the man who looks too far down the path will trip over the roots and rocks beneath his feet. You must be able to do both if you are to succeed. The path will be difficult, but it will be worth the effort."

# CHAPTER FOURTEEN

## Lost and Found

The two weeks that followed Daniel's arrival were perforated with bouts of depression and anxiety. He also experienced sleep deprivation as a result from nightmares, which made his temper worse. During these stints of anger, he would seek seclusion and sit at the end of the dock. He noticed the foliage beginning to bloom as the warm spring sun brought forth a surge of life and colour to his surroundings. When there was a gust of wind, it was accompanied by the smell of fresh water. Daniel would inhale deeply, and he could feel his heart rate decrease as he exhaled. As he continued this ritual, he felt his anxieties subside and what was once forced upon him became a daily ritual in the pursuit of inner peace.

As dedicated as Daniel was to his own recovery, he knew he would not be successful without the help of Uncle Ross and Wade. They were a comforting, reassuring force and he was grateful for their dedication to his well-being. During the day, when Ross was busy working as a park ranger, Wade spent time with Daniel. He would tell him stories about his culture and would educate Daniel if they came across a certain insect, animal, or tree. He had a calm, nurturing way of interacting. He spoke to Daniel with encouragement and never made him feel guilty or ashamed.

One afternoon, during Daniel's third week of sobriety, he found himself relaxing on the end of the dock. It was a beautiful, cloudless day and the water was unusually calm. He was focused on his breathing when the silence was interrupted by the sound of creaking wood caused by approaching footsteps. He turned around and noticed Wade approaching him. Wade was carrying two fishing rods and a box filled with bait and lures. He stepped into a canoe and said, "It's a great day to be on the water. Would you care to join me?"

"You already know I'm gonna say yes."

"How's that?"

"You brought a second rod."

"I always bring two. Just in case one breaks," Wade said as he smiled.

"No, you don't." Daniel raised an eyebrow.

"Hope for the best, prepare for the worst, I always say."

"I've never heard you say that before." Daniel laughed as he entered the canoe.

They paddled toward their favourite spot to fish. The canoe glided across the surface of the calm water; the only sound was the splashing noise created as their paddles were submerged.

They attached colourful lures to their dried worm–encrusted hooks. The lack of wind resulted in an abundance of length between the canoe and where their bait broke the surface of the water. Daniel, not taking this into account, cast his rod and watched as his lure got stuck in the branch of a tree on shore. He became frustrated and ignored Wade's pleas to remain calm. His annoyance, accompanied by his confinement in the canoe, added to his anxieties. Daniel began to panic and Wade's calm, reassuring words went unnoticed. He started hyperventilating and that was when Wade yelled, "Sit down!"

Surprised, because it was the first time Wade had raised his voice, Daniel sat down as Wade paddled the canoe toward the shore. He remained seated as Wade removed the lure from the tree branch and said, "I'm sorry for yelling at you. Shall we try that again?"

Daniel did not respond. He kept his head bowed as Wade paddled the canoe back to where they began. He clenched his jaw and tapped his foot. He scratched his forearm and said, "I need to get outta here!"

"And where would you go?"

"Anywhere but here."

"This is the best place for you."

"I could think of a better place," Daniel said.

"And what do you think would happen if you went home? You'd start doing drugs again and end up in one of three places: in jail, in the hospital, or in the morgue. You've been doing really well the past few weeks. Now is not the time to give up. I can help you through the trauma—"

"What would you know about trauma?" Daniel interrupted.

"I would tell you if you're willing to listen," Wade replied.

Daniel, once again, was surprised when Wade raised his voice. It caused a momentary silence between them before he said, "I'm willing to listen."

Wade took a deep breath. "It's been a long time since I spoke about this, but I think my story will help you. Have you heard the term 'the Sixties Scoop'?"

"No."

"Well, I was taken from my family when I was young. We lived on a reserve called Kashechewan close to a town called Fort Albany. We were taken to a boarding school there called Saint Anne's. The Canadian government said my parents couldn't look after me and my brothers and sisters. I don't remember the reason or how they came to this conclusion, but I do remember the day they arrived to take us.

"I was so upset. I cried so hard that I had no strength in my legs. My older brother had to carry me. After we arrived at the school, they took off my clothes and they cut my hair. They made me shower in cold water and we were gathered in a room where we met a nun called Mary. She wore a thick black cloak that covered her entire body from head to toe. She started off being nice, but it didn't take long until she was calling us names and hitting us over the head with a bible. That's when the abuse began. They beat us if we spoke in our native language. If we talked back, they stopped feeding us and even used an electric chair if anyone was caught stealing. I had it fairly good because I didn't cause much trouble, but then I met a priest called Timothy Warren."

"What happened?" Daniel asked, leaning toward Wade and looking at him with wide eyes.

Wade wiped a tear from his cheek and took another deep breath. "Everyone called him Tim the Tickler. He would sneak up behind us and poke our ribs or grab the inside of our leg. One day, after being at the school for nearly one year, he called me into his office. I sat in a chair across from his desk and he said, 'I've noticed you're a little different than most boys, Wade. You don't play sports and you spend time with girls more than the boys. Why is that?'

"'I don't know,' I said. Then, he stood up and walked next to me.

"He removed his belt, took off his pants and said, 'Do you like boys, Wade?'

"Thinking I would get in trouble if I lied, I said, 'Yes, I like boys,' and what he said next still haunts me to this day."

"What did he say?"

"He said, 'I like boys too.' He made me bend over his desk as he sexually abused me for the first time. It continued for several years until the school was closed in 1976. And I wasn't the only one he abused; there were dozens of us." Tears streamed down Wade's face. "For years, I thought there was something wrong with me. Something I did to deserve this abuse. I struggled with mental health issues, depression, and anxiety. Like you, I used alcohol and drugs to mask the trauma. I didn't want to confront it. For years, I continued spiralling downward and I either ended up in jail or the hospital. As part of my rehabilitation, I went with a group of people on a camping trip to Algonquin Park. I had absolutely no intentions of staying and I ran away that first night. Do you know what happened next?"

"I have no clue," Daniel said, now completely absorbed in Wade's story.

"Your Uncle Ross found me running down the road. I thought he was going to take me to the police, but we ended up talking for hours in his truck. Something just clicked between us and it was at that moment when I began to seek help. He supported me through treatment, and I accepted that he loved me for who I was.

"I learned, over time and through counselling, that what happened to me didn't define who I was. It took years for the traumatic memories to subside. I'm still affected by them sometimes, but I learned the tools to help deal with them in a healthy way, without the use of drugs or alcohol.

"For the longest time, I carried within me an ongoing hatred toward those who abused me. Every time I questioned their motives, it would frustrate me to the point of relapse. It wasn't until I was able to forgive myself and those who did terrible things that I was able to move forward with my life. Once I was on the path to complete recovery, both mind and spirit, I knew that I wanted to help people going through what I experienced. So, I went back to school and became a psychologist."

"You forgave that priest?" Daniel asked, contorting his mouth in disgust.

"I had to."

"Why?"

"Because it was the only way I could get better. Yes, the memories are still painful, but I chose to forgive to give me a chance to live my life without hatred or regret. If I continued to blame them instead of moving on, I'd be dead. It's the same thing with you and your mother."

126

"What do you mean, me and my mother?"

"There's no doubting that you've blamed your mother for where you ended up. You've mentioned it several times before."

Daniel was getting aggravated. He clenched his jaw and said, "Well, it's her fault! She kicked me out of the house. It's the reason why I ended up at Tony's, then Squidge's, then the hospital."

Wade moved toward Daniel, looked into his eyes, and calmly said, "You cannot heal if you continue to blame others for your own failings. It was your choice to leave. It was your choice to do drugs. It was your choice to drink. It was your choice to ignore the signs of addiction. It was your choice to seek another father figure. It was your choice to leave your mother."

Wade moved closer and embraced Daniel, and the canoe gently rocked. Daniel started to cry as the buildup of resentment toward his mother was catapulted from within his soul. Daniel and Wade reflected on each other's trauma as the tears subsided. Daniel wiped the tears away and said, "So, you're saying that I need to forgive my mom."

"Well, if I found the strength to forgive my abusers, maybe you can find the strength to forgive your mom."

"And take responsibility for my own choices."

"Yes, but I don't expect you to do it right now and neither should you. Forgiveness takes time. The larger the wound, the longer it takes to heal, but once it does, the ability to forgive becomes easier. Just remember that a scar will always remain."

"Did your father tell you that one too?" Daniel asked, a slight smile on his face.

"No, but he did tell me this. He said, 'One of humanity's greatest curses is the inability to forgive. However, once you embrace the power of forgiveness and understand its healing abilities, nothing can stop you from living a full and happy life.'"

Having a newfound respect and admiration for Wade, Daniel suggested they head back to the cottage because it was beginning to get dark.

Uncle Ross was waiting for them. He was relaxing in a rocking chair on the porch, a cold beer in his hand. He stood as they approached. "You came back empty handed?"

Wade looked at Daniel and smiled. "Actually, we let it go. But the work is far from over."

"What do you mean?"

"Healing takes time, Daniel, and we've only just begun. Today, you achieved a moment of acceptance, and we need to continue using that momentum and open-mindedness."

"What are you suggesting?" Ross asked.

Wade thought for a moment and said, "Daniel, if it's okay with you, I'd like to take you to Opeongo Island for three days and nights."

"Three days . . . Why?"

"To show you some healing techniques that worked for me. Would you like to go?"

Daniel looked at Ross and after receiving a nod said, "Sounds good to me."

That night, Daniel's sleep was interrupted by nightmares. He imagined Tony Cardinal's foot was the size of a house and it crushed every bone in his body. He was also haunted by the image of his father coughing up a river of blood, his mother paddling a canoe in the current. He woke up several times in a sweat.

Too scared to go back to sleep, Daniel decided to remain awake as the first signs of light crept over the horizon. He tried desperately to rid himself of the details from his nightmares, but nothing worked. He slouched and grasped the edge of his bed. Daniel took a deep breath and saw his journal on the desk in front of the window. He sat down, and after taking a moment to watch the sunrise, Daniel began to write.

*Why is this happening to me? Why am I being tormented by such terrorizing dreams? What do they mean? Will I ever get better?*

*I felt sorry for Wade after he told me about what happened to him as a child. It's hard to believe that someone could go through such horrible things and still be a good person. He's helped me so much and Uncle Ross is so patient with me. I would definitely be worse off without them.*

*I love them like I used to love my dad, and I think they love me even though they've never said it. But why do I still hate my mom? Why was she so angry at me all the time? Why was I angry at her all the time? Maybe she really was scared, like me. Maybe she didn't know what else to do. I had no idea what to do, but I was just a child. How is a child supposed to look after an adult? It should be the other way around, shouldn't it? Could I have done more to help my mom?*

*Wade was right when he said that it was my choice to leave. But what other choice did I have? Was running away the right thing to do? I don't know what would have happened if I'd stayed, but I know what happened after leaving. And I don't want to go through that again. Maybe I have to go back and forgive my mom. Will I ever find the strength to forgive like Wade did?*

*How did he find the strength to forgive? Wade said it wasn't until he found Uncle Ross when he started to get better. I wonder if I need to find someone to help get better, too. Or can I do this on my own? I wonder what Olivia would tell me to do.*

*Oh . . . I miss her and the way she used to make me feel. I miss home, and the beach, and pizza and wings from the Kilt. I miss riding my bike around the neighbourhood. I miss school and Mr. Johnston and going to the movies. But most of all, I miss my dad.*

The sun began to shine through the window, and Daniel covered his face to block out the light. He was about to close the blinds but decided to watch the sun rise instead. The pink and orange clouds that slowly caressed the sky were mesmerizing. He opened the window and listened to the birds chirping. A gust of wind blew the hair off his face. Daniel closed his eyes and took a deep breath. The tension in his body reduced as he exhaled. He opened his eyes and saw Uncle Ross standing on the end of the dock. Daniel started to cry because it looked as if his father were standing there. Moments later, as the tears began to dry, Daniel said, "I wish Mom were here to see this."

# CHAPTER FIFTEEN

## Opeongo Island

By the time breakfast was served, Daniel was able to regain control of his emotions. Afterwards, he happily assisted Wade in preparing for their camping trip by carrying supplies into the canoe. They paddled out just as the sun was creating a mist over the water. Daniel experienced a moment of clarity as the sound of a loon echoed across the lake. But it did not last long, and in the silence that surrounded him, his mind resumed its barrage of traumatic memories. He stopped paddling and placed the neck of his paddle across the frame of the canoe, resting his weight upon it.

"What's wrong, Daniel?" Wade asked; he also stopped paddling.

Daniel took a deep breath and said, "My brain won't give me a break. I'm constantly going over situations in my head and it won't stop."

"What kind of situations?"

"My mom drinking, my dad dying, being in the hospital. And you know what?"

"What's that?"

"The silence is making it worse because there's nothing to do but think."

"Well, then let's keep your mind in the moment."

"How am I going to do that?"

"By paddling. We're headed straight for that island ahead of us. Do you see it?"

"Yes," Daniel said as he started paddling again.

"Good. Stay focused on that large boulder. That's our target," Wade said as he matched Daniel's pace.

After Wade's suggestion, Daniel's focus and determination changed. As they got closer, he noticed subtle changes in the boulder and by the time their canoe ground to a halt on the rocky shore, his disturbing thoughts had dissolved. Feeling accomplished, he turned around to see how far they had travelled; Uncle Ross's cabin was the size of a peanut in the distance.

They unloaded the canoe and set up camp. Wade started a fire and they enjoyed roasting hot dogs over the open flame. Afterwards, when the chores were finished and calm resumed, Wade said, "For the healthy mind, silence can be the greatest companion. It allows the person to connect with their being and find a sense of calm, understanding their place within this life. However, for the traumatized mind, silence can be its greatest enemy because the individual is forced to relive destructive memories and the details can cause them to search for ways to replace or ignore such traumatic images. How did you deal with these thoughts before, Daniel?"

Daniel took the time to think. "Drugs, alcohol . . . anything and everything, you name it."

"And what do you think these substances did?"

"They took away the pain and I felt better, especially the more I consumed."

"I understand completely because of my own experiences, but do you think they really helped you?"

Daniel took even longer to respond this time. "No, I don't think they helped me get better."

"You're exactly right. These substances—even though they are momentarily enjoyable—if they are abused, they can lead to more problems including depression and addiction. I wasn't able to completely recover until my need to consume substances was no longer my priority. And I would like to do something with you that began my journey back to health."

Daniel watched as Wade produced a large seashell and placed within it several pieces of dried material. Daniel asked, "What are you doing?"

Wade smiled. "This is a smudging ceremony. The shell represents the first element of water. This is sage, sweetgrass, tobacco, and cedar." He held up each one and let Daniel touch and smell them. Wade continued, "They are the four sacred plants. They are gifts from Mother Earth and represent the second element." Wade lit a match and lit the contents within the shell. "Fire represents the third element." Smoke began billowing out of the shell. Wade handed Daniel an eagle feather and demonstrated how to waft the smoke toward him. "The smoke represents air and the fourth element. Together, as you waft the smoke, they will rid you of negative thoughts and will cleanse and purify your soul."

Daniel continued the ancient ceremony until the smoke dissipated. He then watched as Wade cleared an area of soil next to him and spread the ashes on the ground. "All of your traumatic thoughts were absorbed by the ashes. I return them to Mother Earth and in her infinite wisdom; she will help bear your burden. How do you feel?"

Daniel, with tears in his eyes, said, "I feel good. That was much better option than doing drugs."

Wade laughed and Daniel joined in. His mind was calm for the remainder of the afternoon. They went for a hike and explored their surroundings. Afterwards, they cleansed themselves in the cold water as their dinner roasted over the fire.

Dusk approached quickly and as darkness consumed them, the night sky provided a brilliant display of countless stars. They stood on the edge of the shore as Wade pointed to a specific constellation. He said, "That's Orion. Can you see his outstretched arm?"

"I think so," Daniel said, following Wade's finger.

"See where it's pointing to? That cluster of stars is called the Seven Sisters. If you look into the middle, you'll see an area we call The Hole in the Sky. It represents our connection to the cosmos. My ancestors would tell great stories about how our people came from that hole in the sky. How we were lowered down with the help of Grandmother Spider. She spun a single strand of webbing, and we were able to come to earth to learn what it was to be human. After we finish learning what we were meant to learn, we go back up into The Hole in the Sky."

Daniel, amazed, asked, "And what would you do with the knowledge?"

"As one spirit travels up, it passes that knowledge to the spirit coming down in the hopes that it can learn from the other's mistakes."

"So, that's what you're trying to do for me, right?"

Wade looked at Daniel and smiled. "Yes."

They remained on the shore as Wade continued telling entertaining stories about the constellations. Daniel learned about the great bear and the seven birds. That was followed with Makinak the turtle, and Sisikwin the rattle. The stories had a profound effect on Daniel. He felt small and considered his problems insignificant compared to the vastness of the stars.

That night, as he slept, Daniel dreamt he was flying amongst the constellations. He landed on the back of Makinak while holding on to

Sisikwin. He performed a smudging ceremony but instead of a shell, he held his father's casket. The four sacred plants were replaced by beer, marijuana, cocaine, and a pill. He lit the contents on fire with a snap of his fingers and watched as the smoke formed into his mother's face. "You are forgiven," the apparition repeated.

Daniel was suddenly awakened by the sound of a motor. He emerged from his tent and noticed Uncle Ross had moored his boat on the shore.

"What are you doing here? I thought you had to work," Daniel said as he gave Ross a hug.

"Well . . . I figured I'd rather spend the next few days with you guys out here. Anyways, spending time with you is more important than work right now."

"I'm glad you're here." Daniel smiled.

"Me too. Where's Wade?"

"Right here," Wade said, coming out from behind some trees. "There's no resisting the call of mother nature." He laughed, and Ross and Daniel joined in. "Now, who's ready for breakfast?"

"Me!" Daniel and Ross said.

Ross taught Daniel how to build a fire. They gathered some kindling and placed it underneath some larger pieces of wood. Daniel struck the match and ignited the timber. He was proud of himself when, minutes later, the warmth of the flames heated a large cast iron skillet. He watched as Wade cooked enough bacon and eggs for the three of them. Wade skewered several pieces of bread and gave them to Daniel to hold over the fire. Once toasted, the men stuffed the bacon and eggs between two pieces of toast, making breakfast sandwiches.

"So, what's the plan for today?" Ross asked.

"We're going to hike the trail around Opeongo Island. I wanted to show Daniel a few of my favourite spots where we can do some fishing and observe nature. Throw in a smudging ceremony after a quick swim on the south side of the island." Wade swung a large backpack onto his shoulders.

"Sounds good to me. What do you think, Daniel?"

"Yeah, let's do it."

Ross and Daniel followed Wade as they trekked along the east trail of Opeongo Island. Every so often, Wade stopped to describe what vegetation was edible and what was not. Ross added to the conversation by illustrating the growth of the forest and the types of trees that were natural to the area. By midday, they had arrived at the southernmost point. They rested on a small beach and enjoyed some peanut butter sandwiches. Prompted by memories, Daniel described his friend, Peanut Butter Pete, to whom Daniel owed his life.

Wade performed another smudging ceremony. This time, Ross joined in. Afterwards, Wade said, "It gets easier, Daniel."

"What gets easier?"

"Letting go of the anger and frustration. But it takes practice. It takes dedication. I learned a long time ago that if you carry around that anger and frustration within you, it doesn't matter where you go or where you live, you will never rid yourself of it. But if you confront your trauma and develop ways to accept it when it is happening, its severity will lessen with time."

"Trauma will always be with you," Ross added, "But it won't control you anymore."

Daniel had plenty to think about as they continued their hike up the west trail. They traded stories until they arrived at a small, shaded cove. They fished for an hour and released whatever they caught. Two hours later, they arrived at their campsite just as dusk was approaching. They changed into some warmer clothing and watched as Daniel started a fire. Shortly after dinner, both Ross and Wade gave in to their exhaustion and went to sleep. Daniel, however, remained awake and watched as the embers slowly lost their glow.

Daniel thought about Port Dalhousie. He contemplated whether he was ready to go home, but he was hesitant to confront his mother. Memories of her anger caused doubt as Daniel traced the outline of the scar on his cheek. He snuffed out the fire with a bucket of water and watched as the smoke dissipated into the sky. He imagined the smoke was his fear and hoped that one day, that too would disappear. He gazed at the stars and recounted the stories Wade shared from the previous night. Daniel tucked himself in to his sleeping bag and secured the opening of his tent. The sound of a loon calling to its mate echoed across the lake as Daniel drifted off to sleep.

The next day, they canoed in the opposite direction around the island. It was a calm sunny morning, and the weather made the journey somewhat effortless. The clear water exposed the submerged rocks and boulders as they glided above them. Daniel saw fish amongst the crevasses and wished that they had brought their fishing rods. They made several stops to stretch their legs and they switched positions every time they got back in the canoe. After lunch, it was Daniel's turn to steer. He rested on the stern seat with his knees on the bottom of the canoe. He placed the end of his paddle into the water and pushed against the shore.

It was his first time being responsible for their direction. In the shallows, sheltered by a natural barrier, it was easy going and Daniel enjoyed what he was doing. Ross was in the bow and Wade relaxed in the middle of the canoe. His legs were stretched out as he leaned against the yoke.

"I can get used to this." He laughed.

"I bet you could," Ross said as he continued to paddle.

"This is a piece of cake," Daniel said, mimicking what Ross and Wade had taught him.

As they continued along the east side of the island, there was a gust of wind. Steering the canoe was becoming difficult. Daniel had trouble manoeuvring the canoe toward their campsite and he was frustrated by their lack of progress. He complained the entire way, and neither Ross nor Wade paid attention to his request to switch spots. They sporadically offered words of encouragement, but they were mostly silent as Daniel painstakingly paddled until they reached their campsite. As the canoe drifted along the shore and came to a stop, Wade raised his arms and yelled, "Way to go, Daniel!"

"I knew you could do it!" Ross exclaimed.

"What the heck, you two?" Daniel said as he threw his hands up in the air. "You barely say a word and now you're congratulating me?"

They exited the canoe and pulled it up onto the beach. Ross and Wade stood shoulder to shoulder with Daniel. "Steering a canoe is a lot like the process of recovery," Ross said.

"What are you talking about?" Daniel scoffed.

"Well, you're the only one responsible for the direction you want to go," Wade said.

"That's right! And if you put in the effort, you'll eventually get there," Ross added.

"I still don't get it."

"Do you remember how easy it was to steer the canoe when we were in the cove on the south side of the island?" Wade asked.

"Yeah."

"And do you remember how difficult it was to steer after the wind picked up?"

"Duh."

"Well, like canoeing, in the process of recovery there will be good days and difficult days. Enjoy the good days while they're happening, and the bad days will require work and dedication."

"Did you want to give up?" Ross asked Daniel.

"Like a thousand times."

"What do you think would have happened if you did?"

"We would have ended up drifting in the middle of the lake."

"Exactly. But you put in the effort and steered us in the right direction. When the time comes and we're not around, you'll have to figure things out on your own," Ross said as he gave Daniel a hug.

"That's right! And you can either put in the effort to continue improving or give up and end up back in the hospital. Which would you prefer?" Wade asked.

"I want to continue improving."

Ross and Wade encouraged his determination. Daniel was beginning to understand their meaning, but he was exhausted and all he wanted to do was rest. After packing their campsite and dreading the thought of canoeing across the lake to their cabin, they attached the canoe to the back of Ross's motorboat. They made it back in a fraction of the time, and Daniel enjoyed the wind against his face as they raced across the water. When they arrived at the dock, they each let out a grunt as they stretched their legs. Ross tied the canoe to the dock and asked Daniel, "Well, how was that?"

Daniel put down his backpack, shrugged, and said, "That was the greatest three days of my life." The three men hugged.

Daniel smiled and said, "I've haven't been this happy since my dad died."

# CHAPTER SIXTEEN

## The Way Home

Daniel remained with Ross and Wade throughout the spring and summer. He continued to listen as they offered him knowledge, experience, and guidance. His daily conversations with Wade became weekly as he learned how to deal with his traumatic past.

They celebrated his seventeenth birthday with a bonfire so big that everyone on the lake could see its flames glimmering across the water. Daniel moved back as the heat scorched his skin. He stared into the flames and lost track of time and thought. The once-thick logs became embers. Ross poured water onto the ash and as the smoke billowed, Daniel said, "I think I'm ready to go home."

Ross stood up straight. "We knew this day would come, but let's discuss it tomorrow."

The following morning, Daniel was already awake before dawn. His anticipation for the future caused him to rouse out of bed. He stood on the end of the dock and watched as the sun appeared over the horizon accompanied by a sense of serenity as hues of pink and orange painted the sky. He was immersed in the spectacle when he heard footsteps. Daniel turned around and saw Wade approaching. They stood next to each other. "I'm proud of you, you know."

"You are?"

"Yeah, of course! I'm proud that you have the confidence to go home, and I'm proud that you remained committed to healing yourself completely."

"Thanks. I couldn't have done it without you."

"There's something else I want to tell you."

"I'll assume that it starts with 'My dad once told me,'" Daniel said. Wade playfully hit him on the shoulder.

"As I was going through my worst days of therapy, my dad once told me, 'It's a deceitful sun, Wade. It's beautiful now, but if you stare into it, you'll go blind. If it were any closer to the earth, everything would burn. If it were any farther, everything would freeze. Most importantly, if you end up chasing the sun, you'll end up going in circles.'

Daniel looked at Wade and nodded without saying a word; he understood the final lesson.

They began making breakfast and the smell of bacon woke Ross. He careened down the stairs and devoured his food. Noticing how eager Daniel was, Ross went into his closet and produced a large cardboard box. He placed it on the table and started removing several documents. "This is your father's estate," he said, opening the first envelope. "The house is paid off and a certain amount of his pension goes toward property taxes and maintenance. The remainder of the pension goes to your mother. Currently, the house is in my name, but your father wanted you to have it after you turn twenty-one."

"Really, I get the house?" Daniel said.

"However," Ross said as he looked at Daniel with a raised eyebrow, "I will not give you ownership of the house until you've achieved something."

"What?"

"Your high school education. That gives you four years."

"But I wanted to move back home this year." Daniel slumped in his chair.

"You will," Ross continued as he looked at Wade. "And we'll be joining you."

"You will?"

"Yes, I've accepted a transfer to Queenston Park, and Wade will continue his counselling at the Niagara Regional Native Centre in Niagara-on-the-Lake."

"That's amazing," Daniel said. He slammed his fists on the table, causing the cutlery to jump.

"We'll leave the first week of September, and you'll be enrolled in an adult learning program to get your high school diploma. We'll live together at the house until you're twenty-one."

"Sounds like a plan, but what about my mom? Does she know what's happening? I haven't spoken to her in years."

The charged atmosphere went sombre as Wade looked at Ross. Wade sighed and delicately said, "Your mother has been in the hospital for the past six months. She has something called Korsakoff syndrome. It's a type of dementia caused by brain damage. It happened because of her alcoholism."

"Mixing Xanax didn't help either," Ross added.

"I'm afraid its irreversible," Wade continued, raising an eyebrow at Ross. "She'll live with it for the rest of her life."

"Is she dying?" Daniel asked as thoughts of his father circulated in his mind.

"No, she's not dying, but she will require care for the rest of her life," Ross said.

"Do you think she'll even remember me?"

Ross smirked and looked at Wade. He said, "From what I've heard, you are all she thinks about."

"Really?" Daniel smiled.

Daniel didn't completely understand the frailty of his mother's health, but he promised to try to improve his relationship with Marilyn.

They spent the month of August preparing for the move, and on the first of September they were on their way to Port Dalhousie. Daniel was excited to be leaving but he felt butterflies in his stomach as soon as he closed the car door. He watched the cabin get smaller and hoped to return one day. Glimpses of Opeongo Lake flashed between the trees. With every kilometre, Daniel's anxiety increased. They passed Toronto, Burlington, and Hamilton. Daniel placed his finger on the window and traced the edge of the Niagara Escarpment. Soon they were travelling through the endless vineyards and orchards of the Greenbelt when Daniel noticed the exit sign for Port Dalhousie.

The car began to slow and the memories circulating through Daniel's mind were not pleasant. He slumped in his seat as they passed Mr. Johnston's house but gained some courage upon noticing that the lights were not on. He took a deep breath and gathered the strength to follow Ross and Wade onto the porch. Daniel hesitated before unlocking the door.

"I think you should go in first," Wade said.

"Take your time. We'll wait until you're ready," Ross said as he rubbed Daniel's shoulder.

"I'm ready."

The front door creaked open and they were greeted by the smell of stale air. Ross began opening windows as Daniel looked at old photographs that hung on the walls. He started to cry. "I can't even look at them. I want to take them down."

"I don't think that's a good idea," Wade said.

"Why not?"

"Because you came here to confront your past, not run away from it. Do you trust me, Daniel?" Wade asked. He placed his hand on Daniel's shoulder and looked into his eyes.

"Yes . . . I trust you."

"Then believe me when I say that it will get easier, and these pictures will provide you with happy memories. Look at them when you're ready, but don't take them down."

Daniel held on to the banister and continued up to the second floor. The door to his old room was open, and he walked in. He looked around and snickered. "Nothing's changed." His Atari was still connected to the television. The Star Wars and Hulk Hogan posters still clung to the walls. His action figures were still in their basket, tucked away in the corner next to his bed. He started going through his old clothing, all of which was several sizes too small. He opened the drawer containing his socks and was surprised to find an envelope with his name on it.

As he fumbled with it, Daniel remembered it was the letter written by his father that was given to him shortly after Keith died. His hands trembled as he removed the letter and began to read:

*To My Dearest Son, Daniel,*

*Today is July 2nd. We spent last night surrounded by friends, as we watched the fireworks from the pier. I felt, however unfortunate the case may be, that it was going to be the last time we would share those special memories. There was so much I wanted to tell you that night. Memories of my childhood, lessons that I have learned and mistakes I made. I wanted to provide you with information about life, love, faith, and family. I sought to guide you through your darkest times and focused on granting you unconditional empathy and understanding as you lived your life. But, sadly, as we both know, time was never on our side and the amount of information I wanted to pass on was too great. This is why you are reading my words today.*

*One of my greatest memories was the day you were born. I remember looking into your eyes as I placed you against my chest, thinking how lucky I was to be your father. I thought about what you would become, how often you would get into trouble and if I were going to be the father you needed me to be. Recently, I have felt like a failure as a father because I am not going to be there for you in the future. And I can only imagine what life is going to be like for you now that I am gone. But try your best to remain strong and understand that my spirit will never leave you. To help you understand this, all you'll have to do is look into a mirror.*

*I have always done my best to guide you through life. I tried to listen to the best of my ability and offer advice that I thought was useful. I figured I'd take this opportunity to continue where I left off. Hopefully, your ears, heart, and mind are listening. Don't be ungrateful for the things you want but be grateful for the things you have in life. Try your best every day and make sure that the outcome is worth the effort. Open your heart to those closest to you. Put trust in your friends and understand that they will honour and support your friendship by listening to you. And finally, take care of your mother. I fear she will need your love the most.*

*Lately, every time I look in the mirror, I see a diminishing figure of who I used to be. The cruelties that have plagued my life have left me unrecognizable, even to myself. All my hope accompanies the words expressed in this letter and that is all I have left to hold on to. I hope that, through time, you can understand what I am trying to say. I hope that, through experience, you will be able to recognize the lessons I tried to pass on. But the most I can hope for is that these words are not only read but understood.*

*Over the years, I watched as you developed into the man you are today. You have so much potential and courage and once you realize these facts, you can achieve anything you set your mind to. Allow yourself to grow through experience as we all do and live life to the best of your ability, because you only get one chance. You understand life like I have never been able to comprehend. And it is this comprehension that will allow you to live life to the fullest and—most importantly—without fear.*

*I also want to take this opportunity to thank you, Daniel. Thank you for being the son I always knew you could be. Thank you for your commitment to our family. Thank you for your support through the most dismal days of my illness and thank you for the consistent quality of your faith and your ability to see beyond your years.*

*You will find, as time passes, that meaning will come in different forms. Some people are influenced by fate. Some use destiny as their reason to remain positive and many believe that God is responsible for life. It doesn't really matter what you believe in as long as you are*

*influenced by that which is pure, right, and sincere. For some reason
or another, I was meant to be your father and you were meant to be
my son.*

*Love,*
*Dad*

*P.S. Give your mother a hug and a kiss for me.*

Tears collected in Daniel's eyes as he placed the letter back in the
envelope. He continued rummaging through his belongings until the
redness in his face subsided. There was a commotion coming from the
hallway. He went to investigate and found Wade holding on to what
looked to be a pirate costume. Upon closer inspection, Daniel
recognized it and exclaimed, "That son of a gun! My dad was
Toothless Will."

Daniel took the costume from Wade and laughed. He went on to
explain the significance of the costume and the happy memories
attributed to it. "He said he was too tired to go trick-or-treating with
me. But he ended up scaring the crap out of me and Olivia that night."

"Sounds like something your dad would do." Ross laughed.

As they continued searching through old clothing, boxes, and photo
albums, Daniel's hesitancy transformed into excitement. They
uncovered treasured memories of his childhood. By the end of the day,
they had catalogued only a fraction of the belongings. It took a further
three days until they could confidently say that all the dust had been
removed, the floors had been vacuumed, the dishes had been washed,
and the clothing was laundered. There were some larger areas of the
house requiring maintenance, but Ross encouraged Daniel to focus on
other priorities.

Everyone was getting hungry, and Daniel suggested they get pizza
and wings from the Kilt. Ross made the run and returned shortly,
steam emanating from the takeout container. The recognizable flavour
of the food reignited many fond memories and just before Daniel was
about to say something, Ross commented, "Well, how does it feel to
be home?"

Daniel finished chewing the food in his mouth and said, "It feels
good."

"Home sweet home," Wade said. "Home sweet home."

# CHAPTER SEVENTEEN

# All is Forgiven

The weekend before Daniel was scheduled to begin high school, Ross and Wade took him to a long-term care residence called Fairview Estates in the neighbouring town of Beamsville. It was a new, multi-storied building with a brown brick exterior. Ross and Wade escorted Daniel into the building. They were greeted by the manager of the residence and taken to an office next to reception. Daniel noticed a man sitting in one of the chairs and immediately recognized Dr. Fitzgerald. He stood up and greeted Daniel with a hug. "Hi, Daniel. It's good to see you," he said.

"It's good to see you too. I barely recognized you without your white jacket and stethoscope."

"Yeah, I retired about a year ago. I don't miss wearing that thing around my neck, I'll tell ya."

"Thanks for coming today," Ross said.

"Oh, it's my pleasure. I was so happy to hear about Daniel's recovery and I didn't want to miss the reintroduction of mother and son," Dr. Fitzgerald said. He sat next to Daniel. "Now, I'm here to help you understand a few details about your mother's illness before you go up and see her."

Daniel took a deep breath. "Okay."

"Your mom has suffered extensive brain damage because of her alcoholism. You'll notice differences in her physically. You might not recognize her, and she might not recognize you."

"But Uncle Ross said that I'm all she talks about."

"Yes . . . that's correct, but, because of her illness, she still thinks of you as a child. You've grown since the last time she saw you and there's a chance she won't know who you are."

Saddened by this news, Daniel asked, "Does she remember Dad?"

Dr. Fitzgerald glanced at Ross and Wade. "Yes, but she thinks your father is still alive. It's a complication of her brain damage. At first, we told your mother that he had died, but this only caused her grief, and she would get terrible bouts of depression. So, whenever she asks,

'Where's Keith?' we usually say, 'Oh, he's at work,' or 'He's coming tomorrow.'"

Dr Fitzgerald continued to educate Daniel until he felt prepared enough to see his mother. As they walked toward the elevator, Daniel noticed the smell of bleach. The floors were so shiny that they reflected every detail of the hallway. There were pictures on the walls of residents engaged in activities and each door was painted a different colour. The edges of the handrails were rounded, and he saw people relaxing by the large windows at the end of each unit, residents and staff basking in the afternoon sun.

They exited the elevator on the third floor and watched as Dr. Fitzgerald entered a four-digit code, which unlocked the door. They entered a hallway covered with paintings, decorations, and pictures of major cities around the world. They continued into a large area with a spectacular view of Lake Ontario. There was a group of residents playing bingo as others played cards. The sound of a movie echoed from somewhere, and a service dog patiently waited.

Daniel's attention was soon diverted when he noticed a nurse walking with her arm around the waist of a frail woman. They approached him.

Daniel watched as the woman walked with tentative steps. She looked confused and mumbled several indiscernible words. Her face was emotionless, and it was not until she was only a few feet away when Daniel recognized his mother. Startled, Daniel observed this frail being with sympathy. He now understood her suffering, and she extended her hand toward him. He placed his hand in hers. She grasped it tightly and began swinging her arm back and forth. "Hello, I'm Marilyn," she said as their hands swung. "Who are you?"

"I'm Daniel," he said. He smiled and started to cry.

"Daniel! I have a son named Daniel. Would you like to see him?"

"Okay," Daniel said, receiving an encouraging nod from Dr. Fitzgerald.

Marilyn wrapped her arm around Daniel's elbow and escorted him to her room. It was pink and there was a single bed against the wall. There was a closet and a bathroom and a small white dresser. They entered and Marilyn turned Daniel around and pointed to an area covered with pictures of him as a child. "That's *my* son, Daniel. He's such a good boy and I love him so much. You see this one here," Marilyn said, pointing to a picture of Daniel as a baby asleep on

Marilyn's chest. Ross and Wade were now teary-eyed. "He was only three days old when his father took this picture. He wouldn't sleep anywhere else and as soon as I tried to put him into his bed, he'd start crying and crying. Speaking of his father, have you met Keith?"

Daniel hesitated and said, "Yes, I've met Keith many times."

"Oh, he is a wonderful father. Before we knew we were having a boy, Keith used to say, 'I hope it's a girl, so I get to chase all the boyfriends away.'"

Everyone in the room laughed. They watched as Marilyn continued to tell stories, the entire time holding on to Daniel's hand. She went through every picture and by the time she was done, Daniel was emotionally exhausted. He tucked Marilyn into bed for an afternoon nap and promised to visit the following day.

That night, he was crushed with guilt, and he resented himself for not being around when she needed him most.

Daniel kept his promise and went back every day to see his mother. They played cribbage and board games. Wade would often pick up Daniel from the residence. One day, he found Daniel pushing Marilyn in a wheelchair in the garden. They did not see Wade approaching and he watched as Daniel hugged his mother and said, "I forgive you."

Wade smiled and began to cry. He was proud to have played his role in Daniel's recovery and was delighted to witness the mending of a frayed relationship between mother and son. They remained with her until she fell asleep in her wheelchair; her eyes were still closed when Daniel promised to return the following day.

When they arrived home, Mr. Johnston was sitting on his porch. Daniel had been intentionally elusive since arriving, but now he approached Mr. Johnston. He explained, in detail, what happened and apologized for stealing his car.

Pretending to be angry, Mr. Johnston escorted Daniel to his garage. Then he laughed and said, "That car was a lemon anyway. When the cops found it, those guys had chopped it to pieces, and I didn't want it back. So, look what I got with the insurance payout." His eyes lit up upon displaying a brand-new 1996 Ford SVT Mustang Cobra in metallic fire-engine red. He opened the hood. "That's a 4.6-litre supercharged engine with three hundred and five horsepower!" Mr. Johnston continued to describe the car as they walked around the exterior.

When he was done, Daniel said, "I'm going to write my beginner's licence next week."

Mr. Johnston smiled and replied, "If you get your licence, I'll let you take her for a spin."

The following weekend, true to his word, Mr. Johnston took Daniel for a drive through the back roads of Fonthill, the multitude of twists and turns beckoning both driver and car. They returned hours later, smiling giddily.

Ross stuck his head out from the kitchen window to call to Daniel. Daniel thanked Mr. Johnston and confirmed their tradition for the following weekend. "Only if you get straight A's," Mr. Johnston said.

"Consider it done!" Daniel said.

He sat down at the kitchen table across from Ross and Wade. He was nervous, not knowing what they wanted to talk to him about.

Ross said, "We're extremely proud of how committed you are to school and improving the relationship with you mother. So proud, in fact, that we have a surprise for you." Wade handed Daniel an envelope that had already been opened. He removed a folded piece of paper. It contained figures he was not familiar with, but he saw an amount totalling $16,384 dollars.

"Holy cow! What's this?" Daniel asked.

"It's the registered education savings plan your dad opened for you. It's what he set aside that has since collected interest. We figured you needed something to remain positive. Something to keep you focused."

"Well, this will definitely keep me focused."

"But remember, you don't get a single cent until you've graduated from high school."

"Awesome!" Daniel folded the piece of paper and placed it in his pocket.

"Okay, that's enough of that. I'll get dinner started," Ross said.

"I guess I'll continue scraping the paint off the porch." Wade groaned.

"And I'll finish raking the leaves," Daniel added.

Daniel was about to begin cleaning the yard when Wade asked to speak to him. He said, "I'm proud that you were able to forgive your mother. I know it wasn't easy. Watching you reminded me of another story my father once told me. Would you like to hear it?"

Daniel rolled his eyes and said, "Sure."

"A thousand years ago there was this rock. He lived a happy life underneath the surface of the dirt until, one day, when there was a massive storm, it created a stream of running water directly over him. He was annoyed by the noise but eventually got used to it. As the years went by, the rock slowly became exposed, and the water rounded his once-rough edges. He hated his rounded edges. Then years later, as the water level began to drop, he was exposed to the sun. And guess what?"

"He hated the sun too?" Daniel smiled.

"Yes, he did not like the sun one bit. But then something strange happened. One day, he heard a voice talking to him and noticed it was coming from some moss that had grown on the exposed rock. He was grateful to have the sun and water because it kept him alive. They remained together for years, but the moss's constant talking annoyed the rock. He talked about everything and constantly asked questions, hoping that the rock's vast wisdom would provide the answers. But the rock hardly every spoke.

"Years later, there was another storm. The water level rose and eventually washed the moss off the rock. As the days went by, the rock started to miss their conversations and endless questions. Alone, he became sad and wished to have another chance to be friends. But the water continued to flow and after centuries of friction, the rock began to disintegrate. Then, suddenly, the water stopped flowing. By this time, the rock was a small pebble. The sun shone and before long he heard the faint sound of a voice. The moss had grown back, and it completely covered the small pebble. This time, the rock enjoyed their conversations and answered every question the moss asked him. They continued their friendship for years until there was a forest fire. It consumed the moss, but the rock remained. But this time, he wasn't sad for two reasons. One, he knew the forest would grow again and his friend would return. Two, the rock finally understood how to be grateful."

"I love your stories, Wade," Daniel said as he removed layers of fallen leaves from the gutter, then the flower bed and the yard.

Once finished, he looked upon his efforts with pride but laughed as he watched as a leaf floated down from the treetop, landing on the spotless lawn he just cleaned. He was about to tidy up when he noticed someone walking toward him, pushing a stroller.

It was Olivia.

Nervously, he watched as she approached. His anxieties were soon relieved when she waved energetically and gave him an inviting smile. "I heard you were back in town," she said. The bonnet of the stroller was closed. She approached Daniel and wrapped her arms around him. They remained locked together and neither of them felt the need to loosen their grip. Finally, Olivia took a step back.

Daniel adoringly gazed into her eyes and was reminded of the affection he had ignored as a youth. He wished he had the courage to tell her how much he loved her, but he remained silent. He hoped she could forgive him and give him a second chance to return the affection she had once given unconditionally.

As Daniel searched for the courage to speak, the sound of a baby cooing came from within the stroller. Olivia opened the bonnet and said, "This is my daughter, Sara." She had curly blonde hair and dimpled cheeks. Daniel looked closer and noticed she had her mother's eyes. Olivia placed a soother in her mouth and Daniel watched as she quietly drifted off to sleep.

"Who's the father?" Daniel asked.

"Remember the time I bumped into you on Clifton Hill? Remember the guy I was with?"

"Chris." Daniel shrugged.

"Yeah, anyways, he left as soon as he found out I was pregnant."

"That's horrible!"

"Nah, it'd be even more horrible if he stuck around."

Daniel, inspired by the news, said, "How are your parents? I miss your mom's cooking."

"Oh, they're good. I moved back in a few months ago soon after Sara was born."

"I remember your parents being really nice to me."

"They still are nice but . . ."

"But what?"

"They get on my nerves sometimes. Especially when they tell me how to be a parent to Sara. Don't get me wrong, they've been super helpful. It'd just be nice to have my own place without my mother breathing down my neck."

"I know exactly what you mean." Daniel scoffed.

"Hey, why don't you give me a call sometime?"

"Really?"

"Yeah, maybe we can hang out like we used to," Olivia said as she wrote her number on a piece of paper and gave it to Daniel; Sara was beginning to fuss.

"That would be great."

"Maybe you could come over and have some more of my mom's roast beef. I'm sure they'd love to see you."

"That sounds great," Daniel said, grinning from ear to ear.

"Well, give me a call sometime. I better get home before Sara has a meltdown. I didn't bring any snacks with me and when she's hungry, she's hangry. If you know what I mean. It was good to see you," Olivia said. She gave Daniel one more hug before walking home. He watched as she pushed the stroller up the hill. She turned around and waved once more before Daniel was summoned inside for dinner.

Afterwards, Daniel enjoyed a hot shower. He wrapped a towel around his waist, picked his pants off the floor, and reached into his pockets. He placed Olivia's number and the registered education savings plan on the bathroom counter. He wiped the condensation off the mirror and looked at his reflection, studying the contours of his face and suppressing the instinct to look away. He gazed into his own eyes and thought about his mother and Olivia. He traced the scars that adorned his face and grasped the sink with both hands. He stood up straight and confidently smiled, and for the first time in Daniel's life, he was happy with what he saw.

The End

www.ingramcontent.com/pod-product-compliance
Lightning Source LLC
Chambersburg PA
CBHW050821180626
46814CB00004B/1392